NIRVANA

GIL HARDWICK

Published by eNovella Australia, Perth, Western Australia

Typesetting, Layout and Cover Design by Site211 Media

This edition printed and bound by *https://www.createspace.com/*

National Library of Australia Cataloguing-in-Publication entry:

Author: Hardwick, Gil.

Title: Nirvana / Gil Hardwick.

ISBN: 978-0-9923704-7-3 (paperback)

Target Audience: For young adults.

Subjects: Bildungsromans, Australian.
          Young adult fiction.
Dewey Number: A823.4

As will be quickly gathered, this part of the story of Alan Cameron is inspired as much by *Tjilpi* Bob Randall among many others as it is by the cornet and trumpet virtuoso of Bert Kaempfert, and by no means least Gottfried Keller's classic, *Green Henry*.

Contents

PART THREE

Prologue

The school social was going pretty well, except they were trying to play *Dark Eyes* as a trumpet arrangement with two backing guitars and the one drum set. The problem was, Alan was playing it in jazz manouche while Danny was playing in country and western, and Reuben was playing swing with Eddie on drums trying to keep it all together.

To make things worse there was this really skinny little kid at the side of the stage playing air guitar as if he were Mick Jagger on his farewell gig, and he looked just like him.

Except he was out of uniform, and didn't belong there.

They'd seen him occasionally peering through the back fence, watching them play footie, but thought he was just one of the neighbourhood kids and paid little attention to him beyond the odd wave and smile in their direction.

But there was something else about him.

When they finished the piece he leaned casually against the stage and taking some paper and a pencil from his pocket, head studiously down started writing on it.

They all watched him curiously for a moment, ignoring the crowd, until Reuben asked him gently, "What place b'long you, eh?"

He glanced sharply up, then hung his head, shy now.

"What's your name?" Reuben insisted.

"Rodney," the boy said, almost inaudible.

"What are you writing?" Alan wanted to know.

"Song words."

Danny and Reuben glanced at one another, then back at the boy.

1

Danny said to him, "You Rodney Cousens, eh? We know you mob, b'long railway line, other side Walilya . . . Rawlinia side. What you doing here?"

Rodney stared down at his piece of paper for a long moment.

"No tucker that place, ev'ryone 'ungry," he murmured finally. "Foster me, eh?"

The crowd was becoming restless. They hadn't finished the set and everyone wanted to keep dancing, so Reuben started strumming Bert Kaempfert's *Afrikaan Beat*. Eddie came in on the drums, making Alan pick up his trumpet again and play. Danny finally joined them by playing the high end strings more or less on his electric guitar, the way they'd practiced, but he wasn't paying a lot of attention. His mind wasn't in it.

The moment they finished Reuben spoke softly to him. Rodney listened intently, then went quiet and sat up on the stage near them. Alan took out his whistle and started playing *Swinging Safari* with Reuben behind him on guitar, then when they had Danny back changed back over to his trumpet.

But they couldn't keep him with them. To let him off, for the next piece they played Herb Alpert's *Work Song*, easy for them and only needing guitar and drums behind Alan's trumpet to keep the dancers going, before finishing the set with *Spanish Flea*.

A couple of prefects came up, trying to remove Rodney. Danny half stood to intervene before Reuben reached across to stop him, holding him with one hand on his shoulder. As the dancers began to disperse one of the prefects looked up, cocking his head and signing for Alan to announce refreshments, which did and they all trooped off into the dining room.

At that point they looked up to see a woman coming through the crowd, her face set. She came straight up, and looking up said, "I do apologise. I hope he hasn't been a nuisance."

She gazed sharply across at the three dark-skinned boys onstage and frowned, not waiting for any of them to say - that they wanted to say - "No, it's OK, he's a really nice kid, no problem," but didn't get the chance, then grabbing the boy by the arm dragged him away, pulling him physically across the dance floor and out through the front door.

The four of them glanced at one another, then stepped down off the stage to follow her. On the way past Alan picked up Rodney's pencil and piece of paper still lying there. Outside there was a fair bit of one-sided yelling going on.

The woman had Rodney whimpering by one arm, and with her free hand was slapping him about the head. The boys waded straight in and Reuben held her arm while Danny and Eddie pulled the little boy away. She started yelling and screaming again as the two prefects followed her out, and a couple of teachers came running across the lawn.

Alan quickly scribbled a note on his piece of paper, then unnoticed handed it to him.

PART ONE

Chapter One

Apart from formally notifying the school, none of them had told anybody they were leaving. The older three had turned 16 last year, Reuben in 2nd term and Alan and Eddie in 4th term, and might have left then but decided to wait for Danny who turned 16 only last week, otherwise he would have had to stay here by himself.

Tribally they were all young men now, not school boys as they were being treated. In showers of an evening Eddie's longing for Valerie was becoming obvious, and they had to stagger their bath times away from the other boys in the school to allow him his privacy, so they wouldn't be gawking at him. Alan's yearning for Gracie was somewhat more nuanced; he wanted to be with her too, but while he knew she felt about things more like her brother, like her father Sam he valued her more musically and intellectually, and for her companionship.

Her voice in mid-adolescence had turned into a warm and inviting contralto, though because of Mum's constant exercises through her puberty now capable of almost three octaves. She had introduced her to Cleo Laine along with Ella Fitzgerald, Sarah Vaughan and Lena Horne early in her training, and John Dankworth, though for his part he still didn't want to change to playing sax to suit her voice but stayed with his cornet and trumpet.

When they were playing among themselves, doing gigs at the hotel, Grace preferred singing Anne Murray, and Karen Carpenter with Mum on piano, Bob on guitar and Bunna on drums. But singing with Frances and Evie they liked *a cappella* harmonies better, or *cantata* if there was somebody close by to accompany them, and often sang Southern Baptist, and June Carter Cash. They were all very popular among the tourist bus crowd.

Mum wouldn't be happy about them finishing school. She wouldn't say anything directly to him because she knew his mind, and anyway the constant arguing over funding and expenses kept them apart. Instead, when he had leave he went into the city to see Uncle Greg and settled things with him; he was his trustee after all, and it was his money not hers.

The other boys had their education funding cancelled suddenly halfway through Year 9 when it was found that Reuben's mother still had a few million tucked away from the sale of her gold tenements, and she had to reimburse the balance. Nobody had thought to check that a tribal woman with a real clue might have pegged out her claims during the early 1960s, long before the boom started; knowing exactly where the gold seams were because it was her traditional country, but it had got out finally and that was the end of that.

Eddie came in, interrupting his thoughts. He had the note from Rodney.

He quickly read it, then rose and got his things together. They were leaving.

He placed the smaller primary school uniform and clean polished shoes he'd bought from one of the younger boys in his suitcase and closed the lid, and nodding slightly to Eddie they made their way down the long corridor and outside. Reuben and Danny were already there with Mr Carpenter. They didn't say much to him, merely turned and shook hands as one after the other they made their way down the path to the front gate, and wait for their taxi.

Rodney had cut it tight, but it probably wasn't his fault. Most likely he was away from there already, and had dropped his note in their hole in the back fence on the way past.

Alan was right. He saw them coming. The moment they got out of the cab at City East Station he poked his head around the far end of the building, then with a quick hand signal disappeared again.

They went inside, where Danny shoved Eddie aside and turning to glance at Alan went across to the male toilets. Bending down, he looked under the door of each cubicle as he went past. At the second from the end on the other side he stood and knocked softly on the door, and it swung open. They went in and closed the door behind them.

Rodney had got down to his trousers, but stopped there and looked up anxiously at them.

Danny watched his face, confused for a moment, then said, "Eh, no worry, we brother belong you. No shame. You look like us."

But it wasn't being naked, even to change clothes; he had no underpants.

Alan took a spare pair from his case that had come with the uniform, and socks and shoes, and gave them to him.

Somebody came in. Danny looked up, listening, then took a cigarette from his pocket and lit it while Rodney changed quickly into the school uniform and Alan put his old things in his case.

Danny turned and pulled himself up to peer over the door, but there was only the one bloke at the trough with his dick already out taking a leak, eyes distant and paying no attention whatever to them. He threw the lit cigarette into the toilet bowl and flushed it before opening the door and slipping back outside, Rodney and Alan close at heel.

Nobody said anything to them at the ticket counter; five boys in their neatly pressed school uniform and nice clean shoes; the one of them small and skinny, in a baggy ill-fitting suit and tousled, uncut hair.

7

Chapter Two

Their mothers weren't to be fooled. Instead of Pop in his battered old Landcruiser Elsie was there at Lake Marnma railway siding in her big Ford estate wagon, with Eddie's mother Veronica with her in the front passenger seat. Aside from a quick glance at the new boy and a brief probing on who he might happen to be, nothing much was said by any of them. Their bags stowed in the back they all clambered in and she immediately drove off toward Home Lake.

A few kilometres out of the settlement Alan wanted to know why they were heading in that direction, and not south toward Ballard.

"Job for Eddie, first. Jackeroo, eh? Few years maybe, he'll be head stockman if he's cut out for it."

"What does that mean, 'cut out for it'? You know he's good."

"Good rider perhaps, Alan, and a good stockman, and he's a good butcher; knows all his cuts of meat. In time he'll make a 1st class cattleman. Uncle Harold wants to line him up to be the manager eventually, but he's not properly a man yet; not responsible enough, and he has to prove it to us."

He gazed at her for a long moment, then said to her, "That's not the real reason, is it? Where's Valerie, where have you sent her?"

"That's for us to know, and you to find out. In due course. And Eddie, if you bugger off the station looking for her the boys will come and get you, shame you properly, probably throw you in the dam to cool your ardour."

"What ardour? What's that mean?"

Veronica turned in her seat, "Mean randy little bastard, orright. Now shut your mouth, eh."

He glanced sideways over Rodney's head at Eddie, sitting there at the other passenger window grinning ruefully. They knew he should have cooled things a bit over summer, but he was cocky and Valerie had the hots for him just as bad. It didn't come to anything, just got a bit out of hand, a bit wild, that's all.

He turned his face back to the front.

"OK, well, tell us what else. What about Reuben and Danny? What are they going to do?"

"It's up to you Alan. I want you managing the roadhouse. It's going all right but gets a bit too hectic and we need the extra staff. Have a think about it first, except Mr Baxter wants Reuben back home at Walilya. He has a job for him at the school, starting off as a teacher's assistant, and to help with the football team."

"Does that mean I have first choice?"

"Yes, if you like to put it that way."

He turned in his seat to look back at Reuben.

"What do you want to do?"

"Ah, sorry brother," the older boy said slowly. "I go 'long Walilya, orright. Better for me."

"That girl there for you, eh?"

"No. Shut up, orright. She b'long Warmunya side. Can't see that girl, 'ave to wait like that Eddie mob. You lucky one, close up Gracie, b'long Ballard same like you. We fella work, save money, get marrit later sometime."

He nodded. "What about you, Danny? What do you want to do?"

"Stay with you, orright. Work for you Ballard side, work roadhouse, play guitar, country and western."

He turned to face the front again, but didn't say anything more for a few miles.

Finally he said quietly, "Well, what are we going to do with Rodney, then?"

Nobody replied, not immediately, until Elsie half turned her head to ask him, "You're not from Rawlinia, not properly, Rodney, are you? You belong to that outstation mob, up there between Rawlinia and Warmunya, that breakaway mob. Government don't want you there, won't help you, that's the trouble, eh? What's the name of that place?"

"Pukuratju."

"Yes, that's right, I remember now. Is there anyone still out there?"

"Old fella mob. No mother mob now, no kid mob. Not enough tucker."

"Where are they living now, the mothers? Where is your mother, Rodney?"

The boy sat there, immobile, his face blank. Eyes glistening he glanced quickly up at Alan, who frowned and leaned forward.

"I think she finished up, that mother," he said softly. "Nobody to look after him."

Before anybody could respond he said, protesting, loudly this time, "We can't send him back, Mum. He was being belted all the time. He was always outside our back fence, looking for us. If he's forced to go back he'll get sick. He'll die there. He needs to be with his own people, with us."

"Alright, Alan. You know we're good. What name your father, Rodney?"

But he didn't answer. He simply shifted in his seat slightly, closer to Alan.

After a long while Veronica in the front said to him, "That fella Laurie Cousens, eh? That one uncle b'long Teddy Scott, mother-side. That mother b'long Yatjimarra side, other side. You father-side nephew b'long Andy, that brother-in-law b'long me, you fella. That Andy father-side b'long Alan. You call 'im Alan brother-cousin, that one, same like Reuben, Danny, but other side from you, orright."

Veronica was the oracle on who is who and where and when throughout the entire eastern goldfields, western Nullarbor and south-west desert country; all of around 1,200 people scattered across half a million square kilometres of remote arid semi-desert. Her word was final. Nobody said anything after that.

Chapter Three

It was a good 140 kilometres across the flat, semi-arid landscape from the Lake Marnma rail siding out to the rambling old homestead and outbuildings of Home Lake Station. Even then it took three hours to get there on the corrugated, unsealed road, so by time they arrived they were tired and covered in brown dust, and it was lunchtime.

A fair way inside the western boundary fence they'd begun to run into mobs of sheep. Uncle Ken had decided off his own bat to sow saltbush and run sheep in these big paddocks along their western boundary, and they all decided he could well be right so let him go.

There was a big woolshed over on the other, western side of Lake Marnma, where the country traditionally carried sheep alongside dry cropping, and he'd brought in dry-country fine wool merinos from the Western Riverina, over there in New South Wales, with a mix of Corriedale ewes and Suffolk rams in the big paddocks further south to produce premium saltbush-fed lamb for the gourmet restaurants in Adelaide as well as Perth.

But it was all new to Eddie, this sheep business, and for the rest of the way had to put up with their jibes about being a sheep man now, won't need to go looking for Valerie, unna?

Poppy Jim was bed-ridden these days. They had partitioned off one end of the back veranda for him as a sleepout, and brought in a nurse to feed him and look after him, with a ramp so his old tribal brother and soul-mate Paddie Miller could come up in his wheelchair and sit with him during the day.

The moment they arrived Alan went up to sit with him too, this time with Rodney close at heel like a stray pup, like his dog Eric, except Eric was fully grown now and had sired six litters of pups. Alan went to sit with Jim, holding his hand and talking softly with him as was his habit these days whenever he came out here. Paddie quickly caught hold of Rodney and was hanging on to him.

Rodney had shed his tie early, and left his suit coat in the car, so his uniform shirt and trousers looked even more baggie on his skinny frame. It was obvious they didn't belong to him.

Half-turning in his wheelchair old Paddie unbuttoned his shirt and poked at his protruding ribs with his bony, arthritic claws of fingers. He held his face in his hands and looked into his eyes.

He didn't say anything to him, but glanced instead across at Alan. Jim nudged him to turn and see what he wanted.

"Ah, that one Rodney," he said. "He little brother belong me now. No mother, eh. Father, that Laurie Cousins, belong that outstation Rawlinia side; Pukuratju, that place. Welfare fostered him to Perth, but no good there for him. He's a bit runty, eh?"

Paddie started pulling Rodney's shirt off and he shied away from him until Alan nodded that it was alright. The crippled old man turned him about, looking at him up and down, muttering angrily to himself, until Jim rang a little bell and the nurse came in.

Jim said to her to go find one of the boys, about that boy's size, and send him to the laundry to bring him some proper clothes. She returned 20 minutes later with a clean shirt and pants, with new underpants his right size now, and socks and good pair of clean riding boots, and a gaggle of inquisitive station boys in tow.

She placed the clothes on the bed and turned to go, shoving them out of the way and closing the door behind her. Rodney stood there frightened now with his shirt hanging down the back of his trousers while Paddie kept hold of him, worrying maybe that he was about to bolt.

"That old man Paddie Miller, Rodney," Alan said softly, "Patrick Patjarrli Miller, grandfather belong Veronica, eh? Great grandfather

13

belong Eddie Cheong. He is your granny, Rodney, from the old times. That one big magic man, big boss for country. This old man Jim Forrestal, great grandfather belong me, my Poppy Jim, properly. These two old fellas are the top Law Men now, right across, properly big men. Proper magic men, two roads now."

Rodney stood there head down in awe, frozen, eyes glistening, until Jim nudged Alan again and he went over to him.

"It's all right, mate. Hold your head up. They like you, alright."

"Take those silly school clothes off, unna. They got some better clothes for you, put them on. Don't worry about it."

Rodney came in close to him, half behind him, head still down until Paddie barked something suddenly in language, which made him look up.

The two old men together were gazing directly at him, but Alan defended him and deflected their gaze.

"He's good," he said to them, "just little brother, know nothing. I'm boss for him, alright."

After a long moment he turned his head back down away from them and said, "Get dressed, Rodney. Don't worry about it. No shame, alright, same like us."

But then something twigged and instead of retreating further, Rodney bent down and took off his shoes and socks, then undid his belt and dropped his trousers and underpants. He stood there, head up now, before stepping across to the bed to take the new underpants and slip them on. He looked down at them, and satisfied they were the right size put on the shirt and buttoned it up, then the white moleskins and brown plaited belt. Then he sat in one of the chairs and pulled on the socks and boots, and stood again gazing about.

"Properly!" Paddy chuckled.

Alan said something to him then and he stepped back across to Paddie's wheelchair, and the old man wiped sweat from his armpits and rubbed it on him before sending him over to Jim for the same treatment.

He turned back around to Alan, eyes bright now, smiling from ear to ear.

When the girl came in pushing the trolley with their geriatric beef soup and crusty, freshly-baked bread for lunch, they sent her back to the kitchen for two more bowls.

An hour later, on the way back out to the car Mum looked at Rodney in his new station clothes, then glanced curiously across at Alan.

He wasn't paying much attention to her, merely nodding across at Eddie also in his station clobber by now, who just grinned back and waved, then without saying anything turned and disappeared from view behind the house, making his way over to the cattle yards to start his new job.

A bit over four hours later they were in Walilya to drop Reuben off. Instead of living in the big dormitory now with the schoolboys, or with the Baxters, he would be boarding with Dr Jayaraman who was still there running the clinic.

Then they drove south through the gathering dusk to arrive in Ballard just after nightfall. The big sky was breathtakingly beautiful at that time of day, out there in the open country, so they drove on without saying anything to one another, and when they arrived said even less.

Chapter Four

Though the dining room was closed the kitchen was still open. As they put their things in their rooms in the old house, tired from the long day Rodney started to strip off his clothes and climb straight into Eddie's old bed, but Alan stopped him and made him come over with them to the hotel and have something to eat first, a decent hearty meal finally; probably his first in a good long while.

Bellies full, he went into the store room and got him a new toothbrush and toothpaste, and a towel and face washer. Back in the house he joined him in the shower, patiently talking to him and explaining the rules while Danny stood there waiting his turn, watching Rodney intently and nodding his agreement, before they all crashed after the long train journey and even longer day in the car.

A great deal had changed over the past four years, since they first arrived to take over running the place. Bob Kelly had retired as regional police superintendent and built a new house closer to the main road where he and Mum now lived. The old sleepout along the back wall of the hotel had been demolished in favour of a shady brick-paved terrace with bistro tables, shaded with sails and colourful though somewhat incongruous beach umbrellas, and with pot plants scattered about it was nice.

The post office and bank at the front on that end was no longer there. The government had pensioned off Mrs Robinson finally and the new people now occupied their own building over there on the other side of the road next to the roadhouse, much closer to the police station. The demountable meat house and single accommodation had also been relocated some distance away, well behind the old house closer to Sam's extensive vegetable gardens. Mum's twin older brothers Uncle Dan and Uncle Harry had decided at some time to move into the house, so Danny slept in Eddie's bed while they rolled a swag out on the floor for Rodney. After years sleeping in dormitories, Danny didn't want to be in a room by himself anyway.

The French girl Monique had long gone, and they had a new Japanese chef by the name of Akiko but with a French husband Benoît and two handsome mixed-race boys they had named, oddly enough, Clovis and Pepin, who were all living in the house as well. Benoît had been a chef himself, but going slowly crazy working flat out for years in huge city restaurant kitchens had decided finally to go bush and find more quiet work as a gardener. In between planting new shrubbery around the hotel, generally he worked with Sam in the market garden, and grew mull for his own use way down the back, well out of sight.

Akiko and Benoît were in the master bedroom; Mum's old room, and Dad's back when he was alive; when they first came out here to Ballard, and their boys shared Monique's old room at the back. With the mad Frenchman and five boys now in the house, and quiet needed while Akiko slept in after her long evening shift, Dan and Harry beat a hasty retreat further south into one of the demountable houses. The shy, reclusive bushmen liked their peace and quiet.

Once he realised the two mixed-Japanese boys didn't get along very well together, fighting all the time with one taking after his quiet, disciplined mother and the other after his wildly erratic father, Alan thought maybe they could have one of the two smaller rooms each while his three shared the big room at the back of the house, Monique's old room, that was too big for them anyway. They rattled around in it, with no sense of belonging. He'd put the idea to them.

Next morning broke warm and clear, though the night had been cold, and they were up early again to find Benoît with his two boys already at breakfast. Eric was in his usual spot on the back veranda, just outside the kitchen door, tongue lolling and tail thumping on the brickwork paving in welcome. In the four years he had sired six

17

litters in all, one of them from a kelpie bitch belonging to Uncle Ken who wanted to see how well the hybrid pups could work sheep, and the rest rounded up by the ranger, impounded, and most likely euthanised.

Grace was there already with Evie and Frances waiting on the dining room, and she smiled shyly at him on the way past with a quick hand sign to catch up later, after they'd finished their morning shift. Veronica caught her at it and glared at both of them, but Alan just gave her his nicest smile before getting up to pour tea all round. He'd learned to wrap her around his little finger, and happy to have him as her future son-in-law, up to a point she let him get away with it.

What was on his mind was the roadhouse. He'd catch up with Bob Kelly later; he slept in of a morning like Akiko, both keeping the bar and the kitchen open until late every night, counting the till and securing the place before turning in. He'd forgiven him for getting together with Mum so soon after Dad died, it was OK, and he was a good bloke. It was good of him to offer to come and take over the bar when he retired from the police, taking the weight off Dan and adding to the reputation of Ballard as a good close-knit community, a safe place to be after all those years with crooked cops and rough working miners, and a nice place to visit and enjoy.

He got breakfast out of the way quickly, and stood to leave in the hope that Rodney would attach himself to the other boys while he and Danny went to look over the job, but no chance. He was the man, and neither of them were letting him out of their sight. Instead he had not only Rodney but Clovis and Pepin in tow as well, though he made them all sit and finish breakfast properly, and not wolf it down and be sick on him later.

Finally they started off, except Benoît and his two boys took off toward the road, while Alan and his mob headed into the bush running parallel to it. They waited a long moment while the newcomers stopped to see what they were doing, and turned around and joined them.

"Why do we go zis way?" the Frenchman demanded to know. "Zis is ze long way, through ze bush. Is difficult."

But they weren't listening. When they reached the graveyard Danny cocked his head toward the road where the newer earthworks and tarmac were still evident, even after four years.

"*Mapun* there," he said softly, "dead fella. That copper cunt. Car blow up, bikie mob, blow 'im smithereens that bastard, no bloody good. Can't get rid of 'im now. We go around 'im, go this way, alright."

He pointed to a fairly plain grave over in the corner of the paddock.

"That one there," he went on, "that one Bad Barry. Pentridge Prison, that fella. Gelignite Jack. Blow 'im up copper cunt, blow 'im up cop car that place, properly."

Alan turned on him, voice raised. "Shut up Danny, you know nothing. You weren't there. Not your story, eh? You shouldn't be saying that, alright. I'm the boss for that story, properly. Nobody else. Everybody knows that."

Danny froze. He was a cheeky, talkative bugger at the best of times, but he should have known better. He did know better. They'd been away at whitefella school for the past four years, sharing a dormitory, and he'd become too familiar. He knew that. He knew that out here he could get a proper hiding for jumping the gun the way he just did, stealing another man's words like that; big-noting himself when he had no such right. Now he owed Alan big time. Deadly.

Rodney watched him intently, taking it all in, but then Alan stepped forward and stood before the grave closest to them. He went over and picked some blossoms off one of the straggly shrubs there and laid them on the gravestone, then stood silently there for a long moment.

Rodney glanced up at him.

"That one your Daddy, eh?" he said, almost inaudibly so only Alan could hear.

Alan's bottom lip quivered slightly but he still didn't say anything, until abruptly he turned to Clovis and said, "Anyway, how can you have a name like Clovis? Doesn't suit you at all. Pepin I can understand, because he's a monkey; I know Pepin became king, Pépin *le Bref*, but they were Carolingians not Franks . . . Benoît . . . you're mad you've got it all wrong . . . to be consistent he should be Carloman, not bloody Clovis . . . different regime altogether . . . so, what's you real name, your Japanese name?"

He took everybody by such surprise that Clovis simply said, "Katsu."

"So what's Pepin's real name?"

"Jiro."

"Right. No more bullshit, I'm tired of it."

Being back wasn't so easy as he thought it might be. He was being grumpy, and he shook his head to be rid of it. With a quick backward glance at Benoît he turned and strode off, through the graveyard with only a brief nod at Bad Barry on the way past, and into the bush on the other side.

The morning was not destined to go as planned. Veering north opposite the road house across clear ground they saw the local sergeant drive past along the road. Seeing them there he made a quick U-turn and came back. He pulled up beside the road and waited until they came up.

"G'day, Alan," he said cheerily, holding his hand out to shake. "What are you doing back here so soon? Didn't expect you until mid-year."

"Ah, we've left school now, Terry. Mum wants me to manage the roadhouse."

"Is that right? Well, you're the right man for the job, that's for sure. Anything we can do to help, let's know. Call in for a chat sometime."

Then he turned to Danny, holding his hand out to him too.

"Danny. S'pose you've left school too, eh?"

"Yeah, we all left," Danny replied. "Eddie working jackaroo on Home Lake Station now, and Reuben up at Walilya, eh? Finished school now, properly. Working man, eh?"

Then the policeman looked at Rodney, half hidden by now behind Alan.

"And Rodney, how are you going, mate?" he wanted to know.

They all looked at him. He stared back.

"What Rodney?" Danny asked finally.

When no reply came he said, "That one Trevor, name Trevor Miller, brother belong me, cousin-brother belong Alan, belong Warmunya side, Veronica side mob, you know that. Been sick that little boy, skinny bugger, look. Bring 'im here now, feed 'im up, unna."

"Is that right? Somebody say one boy Rodney Cousens ran away. Everybody looking for him. Welfare, coppers, everyone. They sent us his picture, look just like that one. Trevor Miller, you say?"

"Ah, all those kids look alike, desert mob. All skinny bugger. No tucker out there."

The policeman shrugged and turned to Rodney. "Trevor then," he muttered. "Eh, Trevor, you know Rodney? You see that boy lately?"

All Rodney could manage was, "Went Perth, that boy. Welfare mob take 'im Perth, eh? Long time, Christmas time."

By then he was hanging onto his trousers, and tugging at Alan by his shirt sleeve.

"Ah, Terry," Alan started, "he's got the trots still. Diarrhoea. He needs to go to the toilet. We were going over to the roadhouse, eh? Ring Aadhira, Dr Jayaraman, up at Walilya, alright. She'll let you know."

The rest of the day wouldn't go to plan either. Rodney didn't have diarrhoea but he did need to take an after breakfast dump, and quick about it the moment he finished he ran out the back way and circling right around through the bush on the other side went back to the hotel, after a quick look either way crossing the main road down the other end of town and coming up to the house through the bush on that side.

He was a slippery little bugger, no doubt of it. By the time the others returned he was hiding in the wardrobe in Danny's old room, so when Aadhira Jayaraman arrived around 11:30 in the white sedan belonging to the Walilya clinic, nobody could find him.

Finally Alan had everybody wait in the hotel. He wasn't there, that was certain. For a while he scouted around through the bush, sending Danny across to the other side of the road in case he was there somewhere, but eventually he narrowed his focus on the house. Going inside he went from room to room, softly calling to him, talking to him, telling him the doctor was here, until he heard a slight scratching sound from Danny's room and he went in and sat on the spare bed.

He sat quietly for a long while gazing out the window, not saying anything at all, until of a sudden Rodney was there on the bed next to him. He'd been crying, and had wet his pants. He was plainly frightened, still trembling.

Alan stood and taking his hand led him into the other boys' room where he took a pair of underpants and some trousers about his size from the chest of draws between the two beds. Then he took him into the bathroom and sitting on the toilet seat held him in front of him and deftly changed him, leaving the soiled things there on the floor.

Still holding his hand they went outside and crossed over to the hotel.

Chapter Five

It was just on dark and they'd come in from an early dinner in the hotel kitchen, and Alan was lying on his bed mulling things over in his mind.

He was happy with the outcome. Dr Jayaraman was very patient and thoughtful with all of them, and anyway wanted to give Rodney a complete medical check since he'd been in her files since birth and she'd missed him in her last two health surveys.

When she heard the story from them of how he had come to be in Ballard unannounced, she was furious. Before taking the phone call from the police that morning Reuben had already given her a quick briefing, so once she heard the boys' evidence she straight away rang Perth to notify them that a formal complaint was being prepared, pending charges of child abuse and neglect; refusing in a clear case of runaway to even consider the counter-complaint of child abduction.

Then she went through a long drawn-out process in a series of meetings with Sam Zhang, Elsie and Veronica, then with Bob Kelly and Terry McCann before another round with all the children and young people there in the small community, until finally she saw Rodney properly enrolled as a pupil at their little home school. As a further precaution she prepared a set of formal adoption papers in the name of Sam and Veronica Zhang and on their signature submitted them, which properly made Rodney Grace's little brother, and Eddie's, not Alan's, though that was a formality they could live with.

As far as Aadhira was concerned that was that; dare anyone take her on over it, so she got back into her little car and drove straight back to Walilya.

Occupied with his thoughts and half asleep by then, Alan was mildly distracted by a persistent tinking sound at the window.

Rodney was tugging at him, saying, "That girl looking for you, eh?"

He glanced outside to see a slight shadow slip away at the far end of the porch, and without worrying about shoes and socks he went through the house and left in bare feet through the back door.

He knew where she would be, so instead of going there directly he made a long detour past the dry creek to the west, then turning back southeast he stepped down into it and followed the sandy bed until coming near their old swimming hole, suddenly she reached out from behind a tree and took him by the arm, pulling him with her up the bank and into the reeds under the overhanging wall of the looming escarpment high above.

She didn't have to say anything. He knew the time would come sooner than later. While the others had had their marriages arranged she had fallen desperately and achingly in love with him. They had been good for over four years now, since she was 11 and he 12. Not yet 16, she was no longer a child nonetheless but a young woman; both of them intelligent with minds of their own, and to a certain point with her mother able to take control of their own lives.

They were a long way from the hotel and its houses and outbuildings. Nobody would disturb them, not soon anyway. There would be hell to pay tomorrow once their ever-vigilant mothers noticed the inevitable change in them, but that was something they would all just have to live with. It would be too late by then anyway.

She began slowly to unbutton her blouse, then stopped and taking him by both hands had him do it while she undid his shirt. She was wearing no bra, and was barefoot as well. She lifted her skirt and dropped her panties onto the soft grass, and pulling him toward her undid his belt and slipping the zip opened his trousers before pulling them down over his hips.

She stopped there, looking into his eyes, and tilted her head up slightly to kiss him as he softly caressed her left breast, fondling the nipple with his thumb and making her moan. The warm soft touch of her silky brown skin took his breath away. She wrapped her arms around him, and after a moment pulled the back of his briefs down over his buttocks. Bringing her hands to the front she reached in and took hold of him, pushing the front of his briefs down as she did so, gasping at its size as she hadn't seen him naked since he was eleven, and he'd grown so much.

Still holding him, she undid the clasp and zip of her skirt and let it fall. She bent forward to help Alan step out of his things, and standing back up straight started to finger his sac and tease him fully hard and erect. Glancing down at him she pulled his skin back, and pulled him in close to massage the inner part of herself with him. He could feel her moisten and get wet, but then he pulled back making her glance up at him.

She stood there confused for a long moment, but then she cocked her head and said to him, "Oh, no, it's all right. My father is a doctor. I know what day it is. Don't worry, please, Alan, it's safe. I want you so badly, I want you inside me. No more waiting, I can't stand it anymore."

She continued to stroke him and he let her, until together they sank into the soft grass and she massaged herself with him, moaning again quietly within herself; her breath quickening.

Suddenly she thrust her hips slightly forward and before he realised it he was inside her, her sphincter holding him captive. His mind zoomed in on the sensation, the experience of it, not just the hot tip of him as he'd always thought it would be, but the whole of him; his whole body was on fire, and he groaned with it.

He stopped again, holding her to him, and she looked at him.

"Does it hurt? I read somewhere it hurts the first time."

"No, it doesn't hurt. It's so nice. Don't talk."

She held one hand up to his lips, and with the other at his lower back slowly began working him deeper and deeper inside her. With both hands around his chest she opened her legs wide and wrapped herself right around him, drawing him deeper and deeper again until he could feel himself now fully against her, the loose skin there warm and wet; her juice wetting his groin and inner thighs, the smell of her flooding his entire sense of himself.

They lay there together like that, lying still, breathing together while she kissed his face and his mouth and his ears and his neck, until without knowing it they began moving together.

So quickly and unexpectedly, suddenly they exploded as one and she held tightly on to him, disappointed at how quickly it had happened, refusing to let him go; wanting and wanting him to stay deep inside her. He didn't want to leave her like that either, after they'd both waited for so very long; neither of them knowing when they'd get another chance once everyone realised they were no longer children.

She began to cry, letting the tears run freely down her cheeks, but Alan only licked her face dry with the tip of his tongue and kissed her, and starting moving and thrusting gently again, until she fell back into rhythm with him. This time it took them much longer to climax, beyond knowing, far beyond anything they imagined, leaving them both soaked with perspiration and tears and their juices and panting chests pumping utterly out of breath as if they'd just completed a long run together.

It was almost as if she woke abruptly from a dream. From some distant place somebody was calling her name, not Veronica but Sam, or Bunna perhaps. Quickly she pushed him off and reaching into the pocket of her skirt took a small handkerchief and wiped him dry, pulling his skin back again to wipe him fully clean, then his stem and groin, loving and tender with him, still marvelling at him; still wanting him.

She stood then and pulling on her panties folded the handkerchief and tucked it into the crotch as a temporary pad, to stop him leaking from her until she could get to the bathroom and shower and change. Pulling on her blouse then her skirt, she lifted her head to kiss him quickly again before she abruptly turned leaving him standing there naked, to disappear into the undergrowth.

Ten minutes or so later as he made his own way back along the sandy creek bed he could hear Veronica yelling at her.

She didn't miss a thing, that woman.

Unfortunately for him, neither did anybody else. Even Eric came right up him sniffing and wagging his tail, and coming from that direction had obviously followed Grace home first. The sharp tang of fresh young lovemaking they carried was unmistakable. The moment he stepped inside the house everyone turned to look at him.

He went to his room and stripped off his clothes, and wrapping a clean towel around him went directly to the bathroom and closed the door. The three boys were there taking their shower, and when he went in they stopped to stare at him, only Rodney glancing at him briefly and smiling quietly to himself. He waited impatiently for them, glowering, until taking the hint the last of them stepped out of the shower to dry himself, but when Alan dropped his towel to get under the shower Pepin's jaw dropped. His eyes went wide and he giggled out loud.

Danny came back in, pretending he hadn't cleaned his teeth yet, and he too turned to look.

Alan glanced down at himself, at the still evident signs of arousal; worse than Eddie distracted with Valerie, so finally he stepped out of the shower and pushing them all out closed the door again behind them.

Close to midnight he was woken by Rodney wanting to get into bed with him, murmuring it was cold. He thought for a moment, then taking him at face value let him slip in beside him. As he snuggled in close he realised the skinny little boy probably never had anyone so near to him in his life, and had simply bonded to him intuitively, without further thought.

Anyway it really was cold outside now, with clear open sky and no cloud cover, and thinking of his own journey through the desert years ago with Eric crawling into his swag to keep warm with him, he turned over and went back to sleep glad of the companionship.

Chapter Six

"Alan, tell me you didn't!"

"No, Mum, I'm not telling you anything. Mind your own business, alright."

"It's all over town, you can't not say anything, to me or anyone else."

"What? Nothing. Flamin' gossip. Let them think what they bloody want."

He turned and walked out, refusing to engage her further.

He wasn't going to be let off so easily, not right then at any rate. Veronica was there staring real daggers at him and he had to sidestep deftly past her to get out the door, but even then Bunna just outside was grinning from ear to ear, and Andy there in the yard chopping wood for the laundry was chuckling as if at some huge joke going around the place.

Only Sam when he finally caught up with him, when later after helping the boys change their rooms around and he was out the back with his cornet practicing, came up to him smiling kindly.

Before they began rehearsal the old man reached over to pat his shoulder, saying quietly to him, "My daughter velly, velly happy, you so thoughtful, so gentle, love her velly much, I no worrying for you. Later, get marry, allight, ev'lybody happy."

"Don't forget, soon she 16, no problem for her, but you boy," he added, chuckling, "have to be 18. Not so soon, eh?"

Then without ado, as Alan stared at him mouth agape, he picked up his flute as he usually did and started playing, prompting Alan to come in with his cornet before Grace appeared next to him almost on cue, arm around him, and with her lovely sweet voice picked up her place and began to sing.

But then she stopped suddenly and they went quiet. "Papa, let me sing it, please, the song I want. I want Alan to hear me sing. He knows it, he can play, please."

Sam shrugged and nodded, and she took her music and opened to the page. She bent closer and said to him, "Play the Louis Armstrong - Ella Fitzgerald arrangement. You know it, and you can sing too; don't tell me you can't." The song was *Tenderly* . . .

The evening breeze caressed the trees tenderly

The trembling trees embraced the breeze tenderly

Then you and I came wandering by

And lost in a sigh were we

The shore was kissed by sea and mist tenderly

I can't forget how two hearts met breathlessly

Your arms opened wide and closed me inside

You took my lips, you took my love so tenderly

She was looking directly down at him, one hand on his shoulder as she sang, her voice knowing and glad, so very much a woman now and in control, but singing to everyone else; her reply to their yelling at her. After singing his part Alan picked up his trumpet and came right in with her for the instrumentals, while Sam improvised by tapping out the rhythm all the way through on his fiddle strings.

The music was their answer to the question, and in it the troubles of the world ceased.

The moment the song finished she surprised them all by launching, voice at her full power as a mature singer, straight away into Nina Simone's, *Feeling Good*, and Alan had to quickly find the page to come in on cue, but he made it. Together they blew it away, challenging them all to say anything more about them, or leave them be.

Before they knew it Rodney was there with them too, with his paper and pencil jotting words down as he listened to the music. As he played accompaniment Sam watched him there with his pencil, and when they stopped for a short break before the next piece he bent forward and took a tin whistle from his music case and handed it to him.

Rodney stood and Sam drew him in close to him, back to him, and arms around him placed his fingers over the holes and showed him how to blow into it and make a sound.

He was good, picking it up straight away. Sam smiled at him.

"You want me teach you music?"

Rodney glanced shyly across at Alan, who nodded and smiled back. He turned slightly to Sam and smiled, dipping his head nodding in his slight way. Sam gave him the whistle, his to keep, and his eyes went wide. He came over to show it to Alan, then Grace, wanting them to start playing something he could practice straight away.

At that point Benoît had his head out the door demanding to know who was going to teach ze fucking school, when were they getting a teacher, nobody here since zat fucking Monique piss off back to France, so they had to say to Rodney they'll have to leave his lesson until later. Sam would teach him.

Alan glanced across at Benoît, and said to him it's OK, he'll do it, or at least get together with everybody to see where the school was at right now.

There were no other complaints.

In the upshot Alan went and told his mother that he simply couldn't manage the roadhouse on any permanent or full time basis. What he wanted to do was go back to what he always used to do and look after the bottleshop, and while he was doing that he could do the roadhouse shop as well, then do the banking and when that was done return to the house this time to teach school.

Friday and Saturday nights he and Gracie would be playing, with her back on the piano and Sam on woodwind, or strings, or whatever. He was pretty flexible. Bob could play drums and guitar when he wasn't busy. Dan could run the bar those nights. Maybe Saturday afternoons they could all get together and practice, maybe jam, or anytime anyone was free. Stop being so busy all the time, so divided, isolated from each other.

Anyway there were reliable enough men with them in Ballard now to organise better shifts on the fuel bowsers, and in the bar and the two shops, and whatever else they wanted to do. It wasn't like when they first came out here, with crooked cops and rough-heads, philistines, and half the place against them.

At that he abruptly stopped talking, frowning slightly and gazing absently out the window, and then simply turned and walked out.

Chapter Seven

As the days turned into weeks Alan started noticing old newspapers scattered about the place, most of them folded on the crossword page with the puzzle half-done in a child's awkward scrawl, some with silly words blocking solution to the rest. Instead of saying anything he buried into his Dad's old trunk and pulled out his good dictionary and thesaurus and started leaving them on the desk next to the newest paper.

Rodney was watching him curiously, but he didn't say anything either.

School didn't start of a morning until 10:30, after they'd all done their morning chores. It was a busy workplace, Ballard, that happened to have children in it, and they all had to fit their lives around the simple fact. This far out everywhere was much the same, either Walilya or Lake Marnma, and especially Home Lake Station which in many ways formed the hub of the far-flung community living on what were essentially tiny oases scattered across the vast arid landscape.

There was no room for error. Everyone had to pull their weight. There was no place for gangs of bored kids hanging around crowded schoolyards between lessons, having to be uniformed and monitored and regimented and marched about to keep them away from mischief; somewhere for busy parents to drop them off on the way to work somewhere, to walk home mid-afternoon or take a bus then wait hours until they arrived home again.

Their little school had to reflect that.

Sometimes he saw Rodney with Grace or Frances sitting at one of the tables out on the patio, pulled out away from the shade to catch the morning sun; their heads down pouring over the morning's paper, or if the girls were busy with buses arriving, with Bunna.

From time to time he sat there yarning with Andy, or Harry in particular with his nimble fingers learning how to plait belts and sew harness and leather. He wasn't putting on weight no matter how much they fed him; still as skinny as a rake, though they all began to agree he was one very clever little boy.

In class he quickly threw the English textbooks out. Katsu and Jiro had grown up listening to what could only be called Japlish from their mother, and from Benoît an obsessively Puritanical Francophone 'English', and as a result were both entirely lost. The two girls Frances and Evie, and Rodney alike, apart from their own native languages, only understood bush lingo.

And Grace, he didn't really want to know about; he didn't even want her in his class but such was their hunger for learning there was no fending her off.

What he decided to do was have them write what they thought, or about something he raised with them, then later had them read it back to the class, or sit with him while he did the same thing, pointing out to them the breathing of it, and the stops and pauses where they had to take a breath, or shift their focus with a new paragraph, and the flow of what they were wanting to say so other people could easily follow them, and reply.

One day during his music practice he raised it with Sam, who after listening carefully to him agreed to leave the gardening to Benoît, and come and help him in class. In many ways he was the real village headmaster in everyone's eyes.

But there was something Sam didn't tell him, and neither did Grace, or anybody else.

When Saturday afternoon came, for some reason or other everyone had found the time to be at practice in the lounge bar. There was a fair crowd there for the weekend off yesterday's two bus arrivals so as it grew close to dinner they had to take their own meals in the kitchen.

He might have twigged there was something afoot, but he was still thinking about Rodney and his potential, and expanding his language acquisition technique; wondering whether they could get more young people down from Walilya to make up class numbers.

He wasn't even paying much attention back in the bar after their meal, when a bus and a van pulled up outside and a crowd of old guys carrying musical instruments came bustling in. He glanced in their direction, watching them absently through the front window, but it still didn't occur to him anything was happening until they started crowding about the stage.

He looked up, distracted and mildly annoyed by them because they were getting in his way, to see Mr Carpenter from school standing there.

He was about to say something but at that moment Bob called him over to the bar.

"What's going on, Bob?"

"Bit of a show, eh? And you're in it."

"Really? You could have said something."

"Ah, you'll be right. No worries. Just let 'em get set up a tick, OK."

But he wasn't happy with that and went back across the lounge.

"Mr Carpenter, what's happening?"

"Mark, alright. You've left school now, Alan, you're a big boy."

The way he said it gave him pause, so he turned to one of the guys.

"What's up? What are you guys doing? What's the show about?"

"Young bloke out this way they reckon, bit of a wanker, thinks he can play Bert Kaempfert," one of them said. "Thought we'd come out for a drive, see what he's made of, eh?"

"Wanker? Wanker is it? Fuck you. We'll see about that."

"Is that what this is all about, Mark, Mr Carpenter sir?"

His old house master made no reply.

"Alright then, that's the way you want it. Know that album you gave me last year, for my birthday; that 'Best Of' album, *Wonderland By Night*? Remember? That one, OK, off the top."

The other nodded.

"Brought your music with you?"

"Don't be cheeky, Alan."

"I'll be cheeky alright."

He turned on his heel and called out to Bob. "Alright, we're on. Uncle Dan can do the bar, you're playing. Get Mum, she's on piano, and Danny; you two guys sit in the middle, with that guy - Sam in front - there on the right with those fellas - the three girls there, got it?"

He stood back. They were certainly set up to play Kaempfert. Two of the older blokes in brass were there to his left, where he wanted them for when he turned to face the audience. He leaned forward consulting them for a moment, to see who'd be playing mute and who was on trombone while he played full trumpet, and that sorted he stepped back again.

"Ah, well, how do I introduce you?" he asked finally.

"Old Farts Band. Think *Travelling Wilburies*, but 20 of us."

Turning to face what there was of an audience just yet, must of them still in the dining room finishing their evening meal, he announced in a loud voice, "Introducing Alan Cameron and the lovely Grace Zhang, with the *Travelling Dillberies*, playing Bert Kaempfert, of sorts."

Turning to the band he said under his breath, doesn't matter, we're good, fudge it we have to.

Glancing at Bob and Danny and the girls, mouthing the vocals for them, stepping straight into it he counted quickly 1 2 3 with his forefinger. The moment his opening high notes came out he had them with him. He glanced quickly from one to the other in the brief pause while Danny then Bob played their guitar bits, but they were all smiling and nodding, all in his swing rhythm.

Without missing the beat the old guy playing mute came in on cue with Grace's lovely soaring alto directly behind him, taking their breath away. She stayed right with him all the way through, as did the rest of them. They all knew it, and didn't miss a moment.

"Alright?" he said the moment they finished the piece. "Big mistake, Mr Carpenter, giving me a whole band to play with."

"It was no mistake, Alan. Let's see what you can do with this."

He stood and bending down picked up a new trumpet case from beneath his feet and handed it across to him. Alan opened it there, and taking out the beautiful new silver instrument gazed longingly at it, caressing it with his fingers.

"It's a Bach Stradivarius. Really? Is it for me?"

"It's yours. Let's hear you play."

"Hell," Alan murmured, "here I was about to punish you old guys for thinking I might be a wanker, for calling me a wanker."

"Punish us, son," one of them said back. "Go for it."

He looked around at them, then nodded. He fit the mouthpiece and gave it a quick blow, taking it up and down the register to see how it was, and then looked up and said, "Alright, *Swinging Safari* OK? Get everyone up and dancing. Then we'll step through each track as we go. Break when you say, else we'll just play through."

"Not yet. *That Happy Feeling* first, Alan. Papa can lead off on flute, Papa and me, and let them hear Danny play, and the trombones and violins. Play it with your cornet, that lovely way you do; that cornet and trombone duet. Let them hear you play cornet first."

It was Grace.

He thought for a moment, then said to her, "Piccolo, alright. And if we're going to do that, *African Safari*, then *Happy Feeling*; make it a medley."

He didn't want to put the Bach down but he did anyway. He could play with it as much as he wanted later. She smiled her sweet smile, her laughing eyes lit up. Nobody complained.

Chapter Eight

He had no idea what time it was. He remembered playing *Stardust* to finish up sometime around 3:00 am with the last of the old guys; hardly anyone left in the bar and everyone else long since in bed, but beyond that it was all blank.

His lips were sore, and his mouth and jaw ached. Somebody was trying to shake him awake.

Toward midnight he'd started to flag, but then reaching absently for a glass thinking was clean water he downed somebody's beer instead. That got him going again.

Sam's breathing exercises from the onset of puberty, Mark Carpenter's *embouchure*, football and competitive swimming, were all there.

They hadn't played sets right through; mostly swapping notes, playing around with technique, talking music, learning from their years of experience. He was a good listener from the times sitting every holiday he could manage with Poppy Jim and old Paddie out on Home Lake, and with Dan and Harry, and Bunna, even Andy; respectful once they'd won his respect, and they genuinely liked him.

About 1:00 am with most of the fellas drifting off, and Mum and Sam and Danny all in bed, somebody went out to the van and brought in a brand new Flip Oakes *Wild Thing* short model cornet with a big flared bell and deep V mouthpiece for him to try. Sweet. Within the hour they were friends for life, and he gave it to him to keep. The rest of the blokes chipped in to cover the cost of the instrument, as they had the Bach trumpet.

He was completely stoked.

Somebody had their fingers in his face, pulling his eyes open, poking him in the shoulder; somebody sitting on his bed. He opened his eyes trying to pull away, grimacing, to see Rodney there peering down at him.

He reached up and took his hand and held it in his lap away from his face. The little boy simply cocked his head toward Danny's bed, and Alan turned his face to see his mother sitting there. She had gone off to bed reasonably early in the night but it was plain she hadn't slept, and had been crying. He'd never seen her cry, though for some reason it didn't surprise him.

He glanced back at Rodney, and said softly to him, "Go and make me some coffee, alright? Make me some breakfast - Weetbix - and I'll come out and eat it, soon. Shut the door, OK. My mummy want to talk to me, just us, is that all right with you?"

Rodney went out, but left the door open a crack and Alan saw him still there, peeping through the crack at him, so he said to him, "Shoo! Go on!" and the door closed abruptly.

Nobody said anything for a long while. Alan gazed out the window. He was still in his briefs and t-shirt, clad decently, but he couldn't be bothered getting up. Anyway, it was still cold inside the house and he stayed warm under the blanket and eiderdown.

"You are so much like your father," Elsie said suddenly, breaking the quiet.

"I'm sorry, Alan, I do need to apologise to you, for my own sake really. I have been so very jealous, of Grace, and I regret that I haven't been treating her so well . . . since . . . well, you know. Seeing you two together has been very, very hard for me . . . I'm not complaining about Bob, he's such a good man, but it's not the same, not like when Stan and I were so young and so very much in love."

41

"I was being perverse, looking at you together, imagining you were him, and Grace in bed with you, not me . . . yes, none of us is perfect . . ."

"You don't need to say that to me. Parents shouldn't say things like that to their children, and what you said to me about Dad, after he died. I didn't need to hear that either."

"Well it's about time some of us did, Alan. Accept it as a compliment. Last night, watching you play, I was so very impressed. You are a serious item, I mean it. Watching Grace, listening to her voice, her singing, her accompaniment, she absolutely adores you."

"But you trained her, brought you to where she is, not me."

"Yes, that part, I understand. But no teacher can quicken a student, awaken a student, bring them so alive like that, that was your part in it."

He looked away, out the window again.

"So, what's the bad news?"

"What do you mean, Alan?"

"You needed to get that out of the way first, mother, so there'd be no misunderstanding later; no recriminations, isn't it."

"Go on . . ."

"No, you, just say it. We can't stay here, can we."

"We simply cannot deal with it, Alan, way out here. You are a phenomenon, and I am unable to contain you. As a business we're not set up for it. It would be like having Sinatra in town. Can you imagine the disruption? You're going to be famous, that's another thing; it's not what you might think: aside from the endless work stress, with you and Grace together the way you are, so young, they will crucify you."

Chapter Nine

Moving into the Highgate townhouse was the first time, and as he thought about it the only time, Alan ever saw Sam angry. It had nothing to do with Eddie, he'd been good. Nobody told him that Valerie was close by at Lake Marnma and he hadn't asked; it was she who found out he was on Home Lake Station, and one weekend she hitched a ride out there without telling anyone, and pretty much clambered straight into his trousers.

When she refused to leave, a few days later some of the tribal women from Walilya arrived on the back of a truck and gave her a good hiding. Without ado they put her on the truck with them and drove through to Lake Marnma, then dropping her off at the school turned around and went home.

With Sam it was nothing like that. They'd found another house for their tenants without any drama, who had moved out the week before leaving the beds and most of the furniture.

What happened was when Alan went into the main bedroom he saw the double bed still there, and grinning turned to Grace made a silly wisecrack about the stud room.

Sam overheard the remark.

He stood there for a long moment, livid with anger.

"*Fut hau seh sum*!" he yelled at him. "*Nay yull beng ah*? *Fah sum*! What the matter with you? *Bahn joo sik loh foo*! I good father! I so good you. *Bak gwei*! I help you so much, ev'ly day. Now I see, you have no good intention my daughter. Shame on you!"

Alan stood, shocked, pale and shaking, face drained, He was lost for words.

Before he could answer Grace was standing beside him.

"Papa! *Hǎole!*" she burst out in rough Cantonese. "It's alright! He didn't mean it like that. *Gie tohng ngahp gohng!* It's chicken talking to duck, no understand. Just joking, between him and me. We are good, we behave, don't say things like that."

Embarrassed and close to tears now, Alan stepped forward, hands reaching out.

"Father-in-law, ah, *yuèmǔ, duì bù qǐ. Qing yuan liang wo.* I am so sorry. Please forgive me. You are my teacher. I have never disrespected you. I never forget, you have been so good to me. You taught me everything. I am feeling so ashamed. I am young and stupid. I love your daughter so much, I will never disgrace your family. It was a joke, between us, a small joke, not serious. *Bie sheng qi*, OK?"

Sam stopped suddenly in amazement, then brushed past muttering, "*Dòjeh, m̀hsái*, allight?"

By then Danny and Rodney were standing there, mouths gaping, staring at them. Rodney came up beside Alan, taking hold of his hand, eyes glistening, gazing anxiously after Sam who disappeared back outside to bring more things in from the van, still muttering.

Poor Sam hadn't wanted to leave his beloved garden, or his peaceful oasis way out there on the southern edge of the vast Central Desert. He was happy with Benoît taking over; he was a good gardener, that wasn't the problem. Nor was it Veronica who was also working fulltime in the hotel these days, spending her time with Elsie and her sister Alice; not much company for him now as age started creeping up.

It was his lovely daughter, whom he cherished and fretted constantly over, and this fine young man who had come into their lives and taken her to hand, beyond all expectation. There was no arguing with him when he discovered they'd be leaving, going to the city to live; back to school, and on to university.

44

By the time he returned from outside lugging a carton of books, Alan and the boys had the big double bed out in the passage, and single beds in from the two smaller rooms for them to share. He had to wend his way past. Grace was in the smaller of the two spare bedrooms toward the back of the unit, with the window looking out onto what there was of garden, but when he saw her there he scowled at her, and without a word pushed her back out toward the bigger one closer to the boy's big room.

The concession did not go unnoticed, a measure of his trust in them; recompense for his angry outburst which was unbecoming of him. But he'd made his point and they respected it.

Saving face is very important.

There was somebody else at the door.

"Right place? Just live down the street a bit, and saw your van pull up. Thought I recognised you, Alan, and Sam. It's Les, Les Cooper, remember me? Second trombone. Not interrupting anything, am I?"

Chapter Ten

There was no time for anything much as the three of them went off to enrol at Forrest College. They all made it in time for mid-year enrolment; Alan on the basis of his Bridgefield Grammar results fast-tracked to complete Year 12, with Grace and Danny a year behind to finish Year 11 and sit their tertiary entry at the end of next year.

It was a good arrangement, Alan thought, because with his entry to university under his belt he could take a gap year next year and wait for the others; get a job and earn some money, do a few gigs with the old guys, see how things turned out.

Where they were living now was fairly convenient, with a bus going past about every 10-15 minutes of a week day, and 20-30 minutes on weekends and public holidays. Going off to enrol that first day Alan was worrying about leaving Rodney alone with Sam, thinking they'd argue all day, which they did pretty much until by time they returned the old man had the little boy out in the back yard happily weeding the garden.

Once they started school again Sam began to take Rodney into Chinatown with him, where Dr Zhang Huá-wei was well known, especially among the old-timers. He introduced the little boy not as his adopted son but his grandson, though nobody could figure out how old he might be. Even Rodney didn't know; maybe 7 or 8, except because he was so clever and having examined him medically, Sam finally decided he was 9 going on 10, but runty.

There had been a lot of children like him about during the devastation of Southeast Asia, in post-colonial Indonesia, and in China during Mao's Great Leap Forward. That such children were still being found in Australia he considered shameful.

The next Sunday he took them all to *Yum Cha*, introducing them all round. For both Alan and Danny it was an experience not to be forgotten; Rodney sitting up there as if he'd done nothing else all his life but eat with chopsticks, sip green tea, and chat with elderly Chinese, and Grace's relaxed fluency astonished him. Alan came away looking at the world with entirely new eyes.

Sam continued to surprise him. He was famous. He'd sat listening to Bunna's yarns, but he hadn't really taken them in; they were stories, and he hadn't fully connected Zhang Huá-wei the soldier-scholar with Sam Cheong the gardener, and music teacher. Grace merely smiled sweetly at him, shyly, lovingly, when he asked her about her father, and said nothing.

By the end of the second week, when they arrived home from school Sam and Rodney were nowhere to be found. Just after 5:30 they came bustling in the front door, Rodney with his new schoolbag chatting happily away, and Sam smiling enigmatically to himself.

He had gone and opened a small clinic down one of Chinatown's back lanes, practicing both western and Chinese traditional medicine, with a small room in the back with its own entrance that he'd set up as a schoolroom; taking children of some of the other shopkeepers in to make friends with Rodney, with a teacher helping to look after them during the day.

In the shower later Alan couldn't help but notice that Rodney's pee-pee wasn't poking out so abruptly now but swung comfortably loose against his sac, hanging relaxed like the other boys as a healthy boy should, not so terse and uptight; that his skin had a soft velvet sheen to it, his ribs not so prominent; his head up and eyes bright and a subtle beam to his face he hadn't fully noticed before in place of the drawn, tight-lipped worry that marked him for so long. When he noticed him looking at him he only smiled.

47

He still slipped into bed with him occasionally, in the small hours as he woke shaking and frightened from his 'bad dreams' as he called them. Accustomed now to his warm touch and soft voice, Alan merely rolled over to fit him in, reached over to wrap the blanket around him, and went straight back to sleep.

It was a month before the new household settled into a routine. With no television to distract them, and not used to watching the thing anyway, the big wide lounge room off the huge kitchen became a makeshift studio. With no car to drive, Alan made plans for a proper studio outside in the double garage, though that would take time. They needed to insulate it first, sound-proof the place, and install more power points.

Anyway it was better for them now. With no chance here in the city to slip quietly off into the bush so he and Grace could be together some times, when they could be home with a few hours to spare from an early class at school, Danny kept watch for them. Sam knew and so did Rodney; neither of them missed noticing every little thing, but they were being discrete, and respectful toward him, and didn't do anything too stupid.

PART TWO

Chapter Eleven

The writer of this story about Alan kept thinking to himself that something literally bad might happen to Grace around this time, entirely naïve about the ways of the world; she not only being the one girl among them but had spent her entire life in a veritable Eden; in a large orchard and vegetable garden tucked away behind a heritage-listed hotel away out on the edge of the desert, apart from a few months away in Lake Marnma with her mother and aunt hiding from a sad and angry *kunmangara* until the proper ceremonies could be conducted to settle it down, and the other bad one on the main road contained by magic.

But no such thing happened. She was too nice a person. It would have been over-dramatic and heart-breaking. Bad things that happen to people are usually banal, commonplace, and silly.

While it took a while to figure out what actually did happen, he didn't want to tarnish either the idea that bush people are capable and clever, merely naïve, and generally unprepared for the bewildering traps laid everywhere in the big city. What did happen was disturbing. It was grubby and unnecessary.

It was alright for Sam because at his age he was an old hand at just about everything, beyond doting incessantly over his lovely daughter. It was alright too for Alan because he'd spent his childhood in a big hotel, and a rough public school as both parents worked so hard to establish themselves, and to a certain extent it was alright for Danny who had just spent his four years of puberty and early adolescence with him at a fairly good private school.

In a big way it was alright for Rodney too, street smart and clever; surprising everybody with his knowledge of back alleys and runs through the city, by which local Aboriginal people made their way generally avoiding the white gaze, the civilised stare.

Apart from seeing them at the stop getting on and off the bus day by day, nobody thought to connect a friendly, high-achieving white Year 12 student with two Year 11 Aboriginal students, the one plainly Asian half-caste and the other black and cheeky, laughing and full of himself.

Not until Rodney persuaded Sam one Friday to allow him to go to school with Alan, and sit with him in class all morning until their early dismissal at lunch time when they were free to go home.

What happened was partly their fault, not paying enough attention to the silly giggling crowd always there at the edge of the playing field, until Rodney walking past them with Alan as they arrived through the front gate ducked suddenly around his other side away from them.

As suddenly they all noticed, and as one turned their gaze on him. One of the girls called out, "Oh look! So cute, what a little darling!"

Danny and Grace turning down the path toward their classroom glanced about at the sound. The girl was up and grabbing at Rodney while Alan walked on oblivious. Danny began running across the lawn toward them.

Alan was walking on ahead, mildly aware that Rodney had swapped around but paying little attention. He was short on time for class. Someone or something bumped into him. Rodney was pushing back, hanging onto him for leverage.

He could smell sex. The rich pheromone odour of it confused him, distracted him. The girl's voice was in his ear now and he was knocked almost sideways in the struggle. Rodney had hold of his arm, pulling him off balance, but by then Danny was there and took hold of her, dragging her off in the other direction.

He spun about and not yet thinking with on hand on Rodney's chest pushed him away, and stepped between them, taking the girl's hand off him. He caught Danny's eye, and together they edged her off the cement path and onto the grass.

Losing Rodney she turned on them.

"Fucking cunt! Fuckin' hurt my arm. What you do that for? Let go of me."

Then she started giggling and screaming at the top of her voice.

Late for class, Alan simply shook his head and seeing Rodney still there on the path stepped across and took his hand. Together they went off toward the classroom, turning back only briefly to see Danny standing there mute, gazing after them. He shrugged and after a quick glance at the girl crossed the lawn back toward Grace.

The teacher was good. When they came in rushed and a little late she paused and waited for them to take their seat, but then noticing Rodney asked Alan to introduce his guest.

The class was 3A/3B Mathematics but the teacher was an old hand, and had worked around the bush for many years on extension and enrichment programs. Anyway a lot of the students were also doing Social and Environmental Sciences, so Alan stood and gave them a quick talk on the Eastern Goldfields and southern Western Desert communities, explaining that Rodney was from the remote Pukuratju Outstation and there wasn't enough tucker out there so they had to foster some of the children and look after them; that he was here to attend school.

That was about it and he quickly sat down again. He still wasn't thinking about anything much beyond the homework he had to complete over the weekend, to hand in on Monday.

Back outside again after only 45 minutes, back along the path toward the front gate they saw Danny and Grace there ahead talking to some of the crowd beside the playing field. As they approached people seemed to be friendly and smiling.

When she saw them approach the girl broke away from the crowd and came forward.

"Oh, yeah, like, sorry," she was saying. "So fuckin' stupid, eh? Sorry you guys."

When they didn't answer, looking instead toward Grace and Danny standing there smiling, she added, "Like, yeah, Alan isn't it. And Rodney, yeah, little Rodney. So cute, I mean, I'm sorry I sort off fucked up, eh?"

"Friends?"

But Alan still didn't answer. He was staring at Grace. There was something odd about the way she wasn't quite looking at him, the way she usually did. And Danny wasn't right either, laughing just a bit too much, eyes too bright, distant.

"Jujube? Really good, eh? Certified organic," somebody was passing him a packet of lollies. "Friends, eh, no worries. Megan, like, she's just silly, you know."

"What? No thanks. What's going on?"

"Eh? No. No. Nothing. It's all right. Just, sorry about before, like. Don't be a cunt."

Alan wasn't paying any attention. Rodney coming up just behind him grabbed the lolly bag and put it in his pocket, glancing up, smiling shyly, but then ducked behind Alan again. Alan was taking Grace by the hand, leading her away.

He turned and grabbed Danny by the arm, leaning over Rodney to avoid tripping over him, and with only a quick glance back at the crowd standing there herded everyone out the gate.

When they arrived back at the house Eddie was sitting on the doorstep, waiting patiently though plainly weary and dishevelled after a long tiring journey.

For Alan it wasn't turning into a good day.

Inside the phone was ringing.

Fumbling with the door keys trying to get the door open he heard it ring out.

All the way home on the bus Danny had been giggling and laughing, playing with himself and being a complete idiot. Standing there on the doorstep his pants were still tented and he was rubbing himself, leaning back against the wall, shirt-front undone and his trousers down around his hips.

But it was Grace he was worrying about. Sweat was pouring out of her. She was hot and hyper-ventilating. Holding her upright he rang Sam to come home straight away.

As soon as he put the handset down it rang again and he picked it up to answer it.

It was Pop. Eddie had cleared out.

"He's here, don't worry. Call you back, Pop, alright."

He put the handset down again and turned to Eddie.

"Take Danny into the bathroom, quick. Get his gear off and put him under the shower. Tell him it's you, it's Eddie, talk to him, alright. Keep him quiet, you know, calm. Tell him it's you and it's OK."

In the same movement he picked up Grace and carried her into the bathroom, stopping only briefly to let Eddie past with Danny, but then brushing past them stood her on her feet and with one hand reached over to fill the bath.

He stood and took her clothes off, glancing around only to see her brother Eddie manhandling Danny out of his clothes and into the shower, then not worrying about it helped her out of her bra and panties and stepped her into the cool bath, talking to her gently as he did so. She was trying to push his hand down between her legs to rub herself with it, with his fingers.

Twenty minutes later Sam arrived home.

The two were still manic, giggling and laughing, but they had them dressed and more or less calm, talking to them, carrying the joke and laughing with them, keeping them focussed.

Paying only passing attention beyond noting the fact of his son being there when he shouldn't have been, he promptly examined Grace and Danny. When he finished he sat back.

"Who giving them drugs?" he wanted to know. "Should be in school."

"Drugs? What?" Alan said. "Ah, yes, I thought so. Those stupid people. That chick, Megan."

He turned around.

"Roddie, mate, have you got those lollies? That bag of lollies?"

Rodney didn't reply straight away, but looking at Eddie said something to him in language.

They all turned to Eddie.

"He said, he's been trying to tell you, but you can't listen. No good that school. No good that place. Worrying for you."

There was a long silence.

Finally Alan said to him, "That's why you're here, isn't it. That's why you cleared out. Nothing to do with Valerie. You worrying for us too much."

"I never lied to you, and you never lied to me," he went on. "I know you too well."

While Eddie heard him, and nodded, he wasn't quite listening. He was watching Sam.

"Papa," he said quietly. "I am a good son. I always respect you. You are my Papa. My sister is like you, clever like Chinese, and like Alan. But I am blackfella; stockman, jackeroo, butcher boy, eh. Teaching me law, country, spirit, family, *kanyini*; those old fellas, that little boy there; mummy - Veronica - your mother Elsie, Alan, my granny Frank, and Paddie; that Miller mob, Patjarrli mob, maybe we know something too, eh?"

The front door bell was ringing again. Reuben was there.

Chapter Twelve

Their weekend was ruined, that much was certain. The five boys crammed into the big main bedroom for the night; Roddie in with Alan while Reuben slept in his bed and Eddie stretched out on a swag on the floor. Danny was exhausted from the manic, hyperactive effect of the drug in his body, and Sam had given him a good sedative so he was fast asleep.

For a while there was a lot of arguing and discussion. There were a number of ways to look at the school they were at now; it wasn't all bad. The academic entry-level classes were excellent, though the rest of it was there mainly to keep some of the ratbags off the street. All schools are like that, it was a choice they had to make.

Anyway, Reuben had decided he wanted to be a teacher, and after having a quick go at it soon realised he needed to continue with his own schooling. He had good results from Bridgefield as well, and it wasn't too late to start with Alan and complete Year 12. Unlike Eddie he hadn't just cleared out, but had sat talking things over at length with Mr Baxter; arriving with letters from him recommending a good study program with a number of fast-track options for the next 6-7 years, until he was happy he could achieve what he set out to do.

Reuben was grumpy with Eddie for another reason, and Rodney.

"You can't just clear out," he insisted. "And I'm blackfella, properly, father and mother. You two mix, you fellas. Not one road or another road, should be two roads; go both ways. Old fellas talking to you Law business to help you settle down, not make you blackfella. You are Chinese just as much, Eddie, speak Cantonese, Mandarin, I hear you talking. That makes three roads, eh?

The two of them lay there in the dark listening, not saying anything.

There was a long quiet. Reuben was right. He had the floor.

"You're a big boy now, Rodney," he went on suddenly, unexpectedly. "Why you still sleeping with Alan? You shouldn't let him, Alan. Already 10 that boy, nearly 10 I bet. Should be cut by now."

"Not yet," Alan interrupted. "Not necessary, later if he wants."

"Well, same thing. Should be sleeping in his own bed."

"You're sleeping in it."

"Tomorrow, change around. Alright? I talk to Eddie father, Gracie father. Enough bullshit."

"What do you mean?"

"I'm the big brother, all of you. Tomorrow, Alan, you move in with Grace. No more worry for these boys, I look after them, alright. They been getting away with too much; you let them get away with too much, don't know anything, not properly."

"Sam won't allow it."

"Yes he will. I'll talk to him. He's worrying about double bed when you are not married, I bet. Two single beds, alright? You two are good, not jiggy-jig all day, not stupid, not shameful. You are good students, work hard, you'll be right. I'll talk to him, OK?"

"Anyway, it's your house," he added.

"That's got nothing to do with it."

"Yes it has. Well, yes, it has and it hasn't. Depends on what you make of it."

"I didn't make anything of it. I wasn't even thinking of it. You shouldn't be talking like that, Reuben, it's no good. Shut up now, alright. Go to sleep. Thanks for talking to Sam, see what he says, but go to sleep now."

Eddie, lying there on the swag listening to every word, said suddenly, "Better talk to me too."

"What? No, you'll be right Eddie. You've been looking after that sister, keeping an eye on me, a long time. But you've been away, Home Lake side. You weren't there. We already had that argument, it's too late now; none of your business anymore."

Reuben didn't say anything to Sam in front of the others. He waited until he and Rodney were out in the back garden planting seedlings, then went out and told Rodney he wanted to talk to Sam for a bit; go inside and do something, alright?

Alan had to get his maths assignment done, and after ringing Pop at Lake Marnma to let him know what had happened to Eddie he disappeared into Grace's room and shut the door.

He had no rest. The phone rang again and somebody knocked on the door to say it was for him. It was Uncle Harold, wanting to ask him a few questions about Eddie.

"No, he was just lonely," he explained. "Nothing to do with Valerie. Yes, he's fine."

He listened to a long moment, then hand over the mouthpiece turned to Eddie.

"Uncle Harold wants to know how you feel about working in the city, in an office, if you're not going back to school."

When he hesitated Alan stood back, handing the phone across to him. Eddie was plainly nervous, talking to the big station boss; he shouldn't have cleared out the way he did, without letting anybody know. But he needn't have worried. Once he knew he was safe the old bloke only wanted to know what he planned to do next.

Eddie just listened, nodding occasionally, saying yes sometimes, until finally he put the phone down.

He sat there for a long quiet moment.

"Where's Bellevue?" he wanted to know.

"Ah, Midland, you know. Where we went to school, but the other side, south side. You can get the train from here, straight there, 10 minutes, eh. What did he say?"

"Ah, give me a job, start Monday."

"What doing?"

"Cattle business, saleyards, eh. Learning cattle buying, sheep and cattle, livestock business, properly."

He couldn't help smiling at that, his eyes lit up and his face split from ear to ear.

Sam came in through the back door and stood eyeing them all there together, Reuben right behind him. He gave Alan only a quick resigned glance before looking across at Eddie.

"Why you so happy? What going on with you?" he wanted to know.

"That Uncle Harold, Home Lake side, he got me a job already, out at Midland. Cattle buyer, eh? Learn the business, properly."

"Oh, velly good. When you start? Monday? OK."

But then he turned and called out, "Lodney, where are you? Come, planting vegetable. You helping me, allight."

The little boy came running from wherever he was, and hand on his shoulder Sam walked him back out through the kitchen.

Partway through the door he half turned and wagging his finger back at Alan said to him, "Better not saying anything, allight."

Then he disappeared out into his back garden with Rodney.

Chapter Thirteen

With loss of nocturnal refuge in Alan, Rodney soon moved into the small backroom with Sam leaving the big main room to the older boys. Still suffering at times from terrible nightmares, and with a few more years yet before his brain reshaped during puberty, he needed a warm safe place to crawl into away from them. The other boys kept kicking him out.

Sam was still working on repairing his thin, malnourished body, making up soups and tonics especially for him, and stretching him out on a floor mat to massage his scrawny frame and build his muscle tissue, then taking him though the same *tài jí quán* exercises he'd used with Eddie and Grace when they were little, and Alan after he showed up in Ballard with his parents.

Most of the time the two of them simply chatted away, Sam enjoying the little boy's quick wit and naturally happy disposition. Before they knew it, coming into mid-autumn they were already bringing fresh vegetables into the kitchen, and clearing musical instruments out into the double garage set up a big round table where they all assembled for their evening meal together.

In many ways things were much better now. Bitten and twice shy, at school they avoided the others and set about completing their studies. It was good having Reuben back, though the house started settling down in interesting ways, with Alan's whitefella way of wanting things to be right all the time, Sam's Chinese worrying over every little thing, and the boys' Aboriginal being in every moment there was to be in.

When he wasn't at his desk studying Alan began poking around in the garage. He got hold of some books somewhere on acoustics and sound-proofing, and went about covering over the small high windows with wool insulation, and the big swing door at the front which was fairly easy because the whole thing swung up on a frame when need be. He got an electrician to come in and install more power points, then he and Danny proceeded to carpet the place and set up his amplifier and gear for his electric guitar. Lastly he set up a good tape deck and CD player, with amplifiers and mixing desk that he bought cheap from Cash Converters.

What started bothering Grace was that he didn't want to be making love with her any more. It took her weeks to get out of him what was the matter. Their intimacy had become desultory, soon over, and he'd turn away from her and go to sleep. Even Sam started worrying about him; when he wasn't studying spending all his time out in the garage now, mostly with Danny but more frequently with Reuben, and Eddie on drums when he arrived home from work, and Les Cooper the trombone player from down the street once he got wind of what they were doing, just playing. Dinner times had a damp mood on them.

Worrying about it, Grace realised that what she should do is study medicine, and become a doctor like her father. It was the right thing, and deep within herself she was very comfortable with the decision.

Always she had been her father's beautiful princess but now she was a woman with a new husband, and she was responsible for bringing it about. With only the briefest of explanations she began to get off the school bus at Chinatown instead of going home with the boys from school, and started work at the clinic. She knew what to do, as Alan had grown up in a hotel she had grown up in the house of a doctor and traditional herbalist and knew all his ways.

When her father eventually raised eyebrows at her, she simply turned to him and said directly, "Papa, no more nonsense, alright. I've had enough. Alan is my husband. It doesn't matter what anyone says. It doesn't matter. It's the best thing we can do."

But then she paused, watching his face. Sam was listening intently.

"He loves you so much," she went on. "He respects you so much, it wasn't his fault it was mine. He is the most beautiful man, he is so good to me. He is upset that you don't trust him; you think he is trying to trick you, but it was my doing not his. And yours. It was you so happy to have him as a son-in-law when Mummy warned him away, and Eddie. It was you who gave him permission to court me. Even when he lost his father he honoured our wishes. He honours me. He is our family, like Rodney is our family now. In all these years since I was a girl he never put a foot wrong; he never did a wrong thing, not once. He has always honoured and respected me. If you have something to say you will speak to me about it. That's all I am ever going to say on this matter."

Sam didn't say anything. There was nothing he could say, or wanted to say. Annoyed at being outflanked, drawn out like that, Grace reached abruptly across his desk and took a pile of scripts, then went into the dispensary to make them up.

They were busy for the rest of the afternoon and late home. Rodney finishing his bit of homework had fallen asleep in the little classroom in the back waiting for them, but roused fairly quickly once they woke him and were out the door.

Once home Grace made her entrance, calling out to Eddie in Cantonese to bring the boys and help her lug the big double bed in from the store room behind the garage, and take the two single beds out. From her no-nonsense tone, and Sam saying nothing about it, without a word they all got in and helped shift things about.

Disturbed, Alan simply went out and sat at the dinner table, taking his books with him, and with only a sideways glance went on with his homework.

That was their wedding. Nothing else happened. The rest of the evening passed normally, with no comment from anybody, except after dinner when Alan went out to the garage to practice the boys looked oddly at him. After a long awkward moment he went back inside and taking Grace by the hand took her by the hand to the bathroom where they showered early together, uninterrupted, before disappearing into their room.

They didn't make love. They didn't even think about it, merely lay together naked, stretched out together in the big bed, legs entangled and bodies together; her soft inner thigh across his hips holding him to her as she talked softly into his ear and he murmured in answer. She only wanted to discuss with him to start about her decision to study medicine, and how that would affect their future together, but he knew and understood in his own way.

He didn't know what he wanted to do. He loved running the hotel, but that option constantly evaded him and he was frustrated with it. They didn't talk about music. She knew already that his talent had always bewildered him; while it was fun to do, for him it was like children playing, not serious. Like a child, it was not something he thought about, he simply did it. It was just too easy for him, requiring no effort especially now he was as much a swimmer and athlete, superbly fit and full of energy, when what he really wanted was something to challenge him and work toward.

And then there was the money. Dad's $270,000 that he'd left him had turned into quite a bit over three million in five years. Apart from the big old house bringing in such good steady rent over there in Nedlands that Poppy Jim had given him as a start-up, under Uncle Greg's careful investment portfolio he now owned something close to 60% equity in seven more houses, aside from this townhouse.

Not least he had the most beautiful girl in his bed, not just some shallow chick with a lovely body but a fine mind and a good heart, disciplined and focused and now with her own career prospects independent of him, who from the time as a girl she had first set eyes on him, before anything else, only wanted to be his for the whole of her life, and no eyes for any but him.

Sometime in the midst of talking about something, some small thing between two people deeply in love; they forgot what it was, they simply nodded off finally.

Chapter Fourteen

Mum had called by to drop her car off, leaving a scrawled note for him tucked under one of the windscreen wipers before heading straight back out to Ballard when she realised nobody was home. Typical. It was Saturday and they'd gone into the city by train, the six of them, while Sam went off to the clinic.

She had finally bought herself a new car, and instead of trading the old one in decided to give it to them. It was in surprisingly good condition. Bob Kelly after years in rugged outback police vehicles had helped her have it set up properly for the desert, with modified suspension and all the right gear, though she had never driven it much apart from her trips into Perth. Whenever they went up to Home Lake they took his Landcruiser. Ray Smith at the roadhouse had kept it serviced for her, and it came with all the log books and service coupons properly completed.

She decided that it was in too good condition for a country car and the trade-in price they offered her would have been a steal, so she left it with Alan; keys in the ignition and a note on the windscreen, and taking a taxi back to the dealer's yard drove the new car home.

Mr Baxter out at Walilya Siding had been giving Reuben driving lessons but he didn't have his licence yet, and while Eddie had been bashing about Home Lake Station in the old trucks he had no licence either, and knew even less about road rules. Only Sam could drive but he wasn't going to be giving them lessons. He was far too busy with the clinic, and keeping Rodney on the track he wanted him to be on.

They were all still out in on the driveway climbing in and out of the car when Les Cooper came past on his bicycle, wanting to know whether they'd be interested in coming out for an old guy's jam later at the old converted army reserve barracks. He couldn't drive either, he explained; had a bad accident years before and suffered some sort of damage.

Mark Carpenter was calling by about 7:30 to pick him up. They operated a car pool, and one of the blokes could drive for them.

Alan's ears pricked up.

After an early dinner they all had their gear packed, and were out the front waiting. Rodney wasn't allowed to come. He was on a diet and a daily routine and had to stay home with Sam. He didn't complain, it was OK. They all knew Sam.

Once they packed their gear into the back of the wagon and organised the driver, Alan stepped across to Mark's smaller car suggesting the other bloke also go in the wagon with Les and the others, and he and Grace would go with Mr Carpenter. They would all fit, no worries.

Underway finally, Mark turned to him.

"What's up, mate?"

"Ah, well, I need you to help me."

"With what? What can I help you with, you're doing great. What are you worried about?"

"Yeah. It's great but it's not great. I don't have my Dad, and Mum's busy all the time, and if I want to see Uncle Greg I have to make an appointment, and sometimes I'm a bit lost. A lot of the time I'm a bit lost. Shit, I'm just a kid, really, me and Grace, we're only young yet."

"Something you want to tell me?"

"No."

"What then?"

"It's like, I've got everything, and I've got all that money, and houses, and stuff; like, it's all stuff, but I don't know what to do with my life. That's all."

"What are your plans, Grace?" Mark glanced quickly in the rear-view mirror, knowing she'd have an answer.

"Medicine. I want to study medicine."

"Sydney. University of Sydney. Number 17 in the world, top medical school in Australia."

He turned to Alan. "There's your answer, Alan. Pursue excellence. Like you say, it's all stuff. With your talent, pursue excellence. Stand out from the crowd, show leadership, set an example. That's what we've been saying to you all the time. You mother has been saying it to you, but you're not ready to listen yet."

"Yes I do. You think I don't, but none of you listen to me."

"OK then, what? I'm listening."

"What am I going to do with all the money?"

Mark glanced at him, then drove on a while.

"Something you don't know yet, Alan, isn't there."

"Like what?"

"Nobody told you, did they? I knew your Dad. I was in the army with him. That's the reason you were sent to Bridgefield, so we could keep an eye on you."

Alan's head flashed up, eyes glistening.

"You never said anything."

"Ah, no, that's not an issue. You'll be right. You're so like him, eh? He never worried about all that 'stuff' either, just tucked it away. That's why there was so much money in his bank account when he died. And he'd get into a mood, worry about the people around him;

get depressed, wanting everything to be right. That's what you do need to watch, son."

"Am I right, Grace? You know him better than anybody, I bet." He glanced in the rear-view mirror again.

"Yes."

"You are lovers, aren't you? It's OK, I won't tell anyone."

"Yes."

"What about it?" Alan wanted to know, cautious now.

"So like Stan. You know, he had a girlfriend, just like you Grace; so pretty, and so graceful and intelligent. It's spooky, seeing you two like this. Her name was Myat. She died in a mortar attack. It was her village. We were the first in and had to secure the area, clean up the mess."

He glanced at Alan who was staring out the window. At the sudden quiet he turned to gaze across at him again. His cheeks were glistening with tears, but he didn't say anything. He just sat looking at him, waiting for him to continue.

"At your Dad's funeral, I know because I was there; you didn't see me. Major Hayes, Darren Hayes, spoke of traumatic stress disorder. That's what it was. He and Myat were so very much in love, and seeing her there like that . . . you know . . . he simply couldn't deal with it. He was in care for a very, very long time. Then he met your Mum on the plane coming in from Singapore, so we all thought he'd be right after that."

"It was, for a good long while. In the end, I thought, he went the way he did because he wanted to be with Myat. That's something you might want to understand; sort of, complete the picture, right? I've known you, Alan, since you were a baby. I was at your christening. But it never goes away, really. Some other cunt coming in, tipping the apple cart over again, upsetting everything, just because of some bullshit, and it's all on again."

Alan was fully alert.

"What are you telling me, Mr Carpenter?"

"I'm not telling you anything, Alan. You asked me to help you and I'm helping you. What else do you want to know?"

"I didn't mean like that. That's not what I meant at all. You shouldn't have told me those things, and Grace and me is none of your fucking business."

But then he glanced sharply away, as if suddenly realising something. He turned and spoke directly to him, accusing him. "You set up Barry Devlin. It was you, wasn't it? You and Ken; Uncle Ken."

"Ah, Barry set himself up. They didn't call him Bad Barry for nothing. Mad Barry more like it. He got just what he deserved, and so did Jack Fucking Hanley. It's over, that bit; finished. It was surgical, excising a cancer. People die and are buried, and the next generation comes along. If we'd done that in a lot of wars it would have saved millions of lives, and protected the culture, and the buildings and the art and the treasures; the universities and the hospitals. The question is, Alan, what do you want to do with your life?"

"That's what the fuck I asked you in the first place! Enough of the explanations, alright!"

"No, Alan. If you don't want to be worrying about stuff, don't worry about it. Play your music. Be a good guy. Be excellent. Be a good person in the world. Be a leader. Set an example."

"So you bastards can be let off the hook?"

"No, Alan, it's not like that. We are background. We're here now anyway. What do you want to play, you're the man."

"Blues. And fuck you too."

He heard Sam speaking quietly to him. He had no idea what time it was. Rodney was sitting on the end of the bed; he knew it was him he could feel the weight and shape of his skinny bottom, his bony bum, and Grace was holding his hand.

He was smiling. The night had been brilliant. When they got home the stars were shining.

He turned over toward them and opened his eyes, glancing from one to the other.

"Ah, yes," he said quietly, almost to himself. "Now I know. It's alright."

He sat up, and reaching forward grabbed Rodney by the arm and pulled him down onto the bed beside him. He rolled over and with one hand pulled the blanket aside, then with the other tucked him in.

Then he took hold of Grace and doing the same with her tucked her in on his other side, like three kids in the bed.

An arm around each of their shoulders he looked up and said to Sam, "OK, *yuèfù. Dòjeh, m̀hsái*. I'll talk to you later. I want to talk to my wife now, and my friend."

Chapter Fifteen

Rodney was well past his old therapeutic feeding with formula and peanut, milk powder and honey plumpy when he was little. His body was digesting food. What Sam now sought to achieve with him was firstly to stop his system feeding off itself whenever he became frightened and skipped meals, and secondly to build up reasonable adipose fat deposits in preparation for the inevitable growth spurt in a couple of years' time.

But he was also making sure he ate lots of soup, with tofu and fresh vegetables as well as meat every evening, and a lot of fresh fruit. What he really needed right now was plenty of work and plenty of exercise to build up his muscle bulk as much as his strength, and with it his confidence. He had him digging in the garden alright; pushing the barrow about, shovelling and raking, turning over compost, enough to get a sweat up some days. What he wanted the boys to help him with was plenty of football and running around on the oval near the house.

With late autumn and spring soon upon them that was easily done. They merely had to shift their bus schedule around, since Rodney was scared of travelling alone so publicly and anyway Grace had to get off at that Chinatown stop to work in the clinic after school. When she got off they all did and waited there while Alan went with her to the clinic and came back with Rodney, and they all boarded the next bus that came along and proceeded home.

That allowed them a good hour and a half running around outside, the five boys, once they'd eaten something for afternoon smoko to refill their insatiable energy tanks, mostly leftover rice and delicious meat gravy from dinner last night, and fruit.

The desert boys out on the footie oval were agile and fast. Thousands of years of oral, non-literate culture, chasing game, spearing kangaroos, had bred into them an uncanny ability to read the terrain and anticipate every move, and with the most subtle hand signals and body language work in concert to thwart it. Alan thought he was the far better strategic thinker, more logical and focussed, and certainly the better kick over the long distance, but they taught him his lesson time and again. Rodney laughed out loud every time they topped him. It was great fun.

Within a week or so a good dozen or more of the local neighbourhood boys joined in, so they split into 9-a-side teams and played match play instead of just fooling about kicking the ball around. Every evening now they came in hot and sweaty, or cold and covered in mud depending on the weather, and jostled each other into the shower. Usually they got Danny then Eddie through first, then Alan with Rodney, and last Reuben. Rodney was a big boy now, and Sam smiled and nodded when he saw him so happy and smiling, so full of beans. That's what he wanted.

And Grace was more beautiful day by day, her pretty almond eyes laughing and dancing as she went about her work at the clinic.

They couldn't exactly find anyone who wanted to teach them to drive the car, so they hired a driving instructor, somebody they found online who turned out to be pretty good. Whoever's turn it was for the driving lesson just had to miss out on footie that day. By late October Reuben and Eddie and Alan all had their P-plates. That was fun too.

Mark Carpenter bided his time. He'd played his hand and sat back waiting to see what the gambit would yield. Alan appeared to have cottoned onto the cosmic joke finally, though that he expected. He was very like his Dad. What he wanted was their end-of-year school results.

When Grace sailed straight through right on track for an Exhibition at the end of next year he sat back in his seat. He should have seen that coming, and it made him reflect on his prejudices. And schooling and access pathways. Even Reuben topped Alan on aggregate, except Alan scored much better in the core academic disciplines as he did anticipate, whereas Reuben had opted for the elective streams in biology, and Social and Environmental Sciences rather than Mathematics, Physics and Chemistry. With their scores both boys could get straight into Sydney or Monash in the first round of offers, it wasn't a problem.

Danny was alright too, well better than average, showing steady focus and effort. If he stayed on that track he would certainly be close to Reuben and Alan by the time he sat his final exams. And little Rodney, just completing Year 6. He'd have to ask Sam one day what was his secret.

In the event he didn't get much of a chance. The boys held an end-of-year gig with the old fellas to celebrate their results, and after a couple of beers Alan turned to him suddenly and told him to piss off, he didn't like him and he didn't appreciate what he represented; he wasn't a teacher and never taught him anything just a school master, the house head; he wasn't part of his family but he presumed so much, and he didn't want to see him around the place any more.

Chapter Sixteen

Alan's plan for a gap year to wait for Grace and Danny, and all the things he was going to do with his time, came to nothing. Reuben was on track and he wanted to go straight ahead. They'd had plenty of adventure in their lives, there was no reason to wait; it wasn't as if they were city kids emerging blinking and confused into the real world from noses in their books, from the education tunnel they'd been cooped up in for 12 whole years; some of them who'd started in day care even longer.

It was OK. Back when he'd decided that's what he wanted to do; before Reuben and Eddie showed up again when they weren't rightly supposed to, he was far more worried about starting university by himself, getting lost in the crowd. More than anything at the time he wanted to be with Grace, and hadn't been thinking about much else anyway. Right now the fly in the ointment was Valerie.

Eddie had to work over summer, getting only two weeks off at Christmas. Sam was busy with the clinic. Danny couldn't be bothered going all the way back out into the desert. He'd be away at school in the city pretty much since he was eleven. He liked it here now, having formed his own group of friends at college, and they planned to summer out at Rottnest and do all the things ordinary Perth kids did.

That left Rodney torn between staying with Sam and going with Alan. The little boy in him prevailed, when at the last minute after agreeing to stay with Sam, as the car backed out of the driveway he ran out with a bag quickly packed and jumped in with them. Sam only smiled after him and waved them off.

Reuben proved his worth, as a good driver and a good guy. He was missing his country a lot, and with the strain of inexperienced drivers having to concentrate for so long, over such a great distance, they stopped a lot to stretch their legs, take a pee, swap drivers, and generally be out away from the city. As a result it took them two full days to get there, not the usual day and a half with overnight stop. When they did stop to camp for the night, well into the beautiful mulga and salmon gum country by then, he was happy to roll a swag out on the ground beside the car while the others folded the back seats down and slept inside.

The moment they arrived in Ballard Valerie came hurrying out looking for Eddie. She was supposed to be in Lake Marnma, and became extremely upset when she found out he wasn't with them. She ran back inside crying. By morning she had cleared out, and all Alan could think was they shouldn't have been so rough on her. They all knew where she was headed, and when an argument ensured he stepped in and loudly told everyone to mind their own fucking business, he was tired of it.

He went into the office and rang Sam, telling him Valerie was on her way and keep an eye out for her. She might be hitch-hiking, or she might only have hiked back up to Lake Marnma in which case she'd be on the train. More likely she'd be on the train, eh?

Then he thought for a moment, and hanging up rang through to Lake Marnma, to talk to Pop but Nanna answered instead. The train won't be coming through for another two hours yet. She'll be there, for certain. Pack some things for her, and when you see her give her some money, pay for the ticket, and when she's away safely ring back and let me know. I'll call Sam and get him to pick her up at City East station.

"What are you doing, Alan," his mother wanted to know. She was standing in the doorway, arms folded, watching him.

"What should have been done in the first place. I'm not arguing with you mother. And tell that Mr Carpenter to stay away from me, keep his distance. Or there'll be big trouble I tell you."

"What does this have to do with him?"

"This bit, nothing. Nothing to do with Valerie, or Eddie."

"What then?"

"Ah, Mum, you know, he told me about Myat. He shouldn't have told me that. I didn't need to know about it."

"Myat? Who is Myat? What on earth are you talking about?"

"What? Don't you know either? Don't tell me you don't know. I'm sorry, I shouldn't have said anything. I, um, I thought, you know, he might have said something. Fucking people with big mouths, they ought to learn to shut the fuck up about some things."

"Alan, who is Myat. And kindly don't swear in front of me, if you don't mind. What has this to do with anything?"

"Sorry. Um, she was Dad's girlfriend, during the war; his wife. She was killed in a mortar attack and they had to clean the mess up. That's what was wrong with Dad all those years."

"You're not serious."

"Yes, I am. Mum I'm sorry, I thought you knew. I was angry with you for not telling me first, that it was some arrogant prick like that shooting his mouth off. I just asked him to help me with something, but that's what he came out with, like he was my new Dad or something."

She was staring out the window by them, off into the distance. "That poor, poor man," she was saying.

"No he's not, he's a prick. I can see that bastard now for what he is. I don't want him coming anywhere near me."

"No, that's not true, Alan. You mustn't say things like that. Your father was such a good man, he loved me very much. I never felt betrayed by him, nor second fiddle to somebody else, not ever. It wasn't like that at all. He was totally devoted to you, he loved you very much, Alan."

"What? No." He was angry and crying, the tears had started and he found it difficult to speak. "That Mr Carpenter . . . that's who I meant. Not Dad."

But there was a scratching at the door. It was Bunna, listening. They turned to him.

"Ah, sorry missus. Sorry to interrupt. Sorry son. Phone call for you from Lake Marnma."

Alan looked down suddenly to see the handset still in his hand.

"Oh, yeah, what? Pop, is it?"

"Yeah, said ter let yer know Valerie's there OK. She'll be right, all sorted."

"Yes, Alan, that is what we were discussing," his mother said. "What have you done?"

"Nothing, Mum, now we're back onto that subject. She's 18 already, for crying out loud. I know Eddie's not 18 yet but it won't be long. Me and Grace are together so why can't they? Hell, they've been married since she was seven."

"Ah, you and Grace is it?"

"Yes. And it's none of your business. I didn't come out here for this. We only wanted to have a nice Christmas. I'm going up to see Poppy Jim, then I'll decide what next."

She watched his face for a long moment, recognising his decision.

"That may be a good idea," she said to him finally. "Yes, he's been very ill. He's been asking after you. He doesn't have long to go, Alan. He'll be so happy to see you."

He nodded, imperceptibly almost, as if to himself, then he looked up at Bunna.

"What else?"

"Ah, if yer don't mind, just do me a favour, alright. Don't say anything to Sam that yer know about Myat. We'll sort it. And sorry missus, it was just one of those things."

"No need for you to apologise, Darren," Mum said. "You of all people."

But Alan was persistent.

"What else, Bunna."

"Ah, nah, don't worry about it. It'll be right, we'll sort it."

"Sort bloody what? Tell me, Major Hayes, sir. Why was Mr Carpenter hanging around all the time, and I never saw him or remember him from anywhere, except school? What was he saying to me about all that?"

"No, Alan," he said. His voice shifted, commanding, the old Special Forces major coming to the fore. "Mate, I tell you, live the good life you have. That's what it's all about, otherwise it's all pointless, all in vain. Honour your Dad by making something of what he left you. We'll deal with Carpenter. You're right, he should have kept his trap shut, but it's our business, not yours."

He turned abruptly and disappeared along the passage.

Instead of unpacking the van they simply reloaded their overnight things and left straight away, taking the long way around via Walilya to drop Reuben off.

Chapter Seventeen

There didn't seem to be anybody around. It was just after mid-day and it was hot. The station dogs didn't even bark, and recognising the car didn't bother running out to chase it beyond a quick stretch and a yawn before flopping back down in the shade.

Uncle Ken appeared at the back door, and then the nurse stepped out of the sleepout to see who it was. Mounting the steps Alan glanced only briefly at Ken, who merely cocked his head to one side indicating he might come in for a yarn once old Jimmie was done with him. He didn't need to ask how he was.

The nurse smiled at him, then stood aside slightly, holding the door ajar.

Paddie was there in his wheelchair. He must have been dozing in the heat, there under the ceiling fan the way his body was slumped, arms and legs spread to catch the cool, but his head was up sharp and his eyes alert looking at Alan the moment he came into the room. He turned a little seeing Grace there, then when Rodney came in behind them his old face broke into a broad grin.

The little boy stepped quickly across to stand right in front of him, and Paddie took him by both hands and held him there, looking him up and down without saying anything. Rodney climbed up on his knee and despite the heat leaned back against him, not saying anything either.

Poppy Jim was on the bed, naked, on a clean sheet with only a towel across his loins and his head and shoulders propped up on pillows. He was skeletal almost, his chest sunken and his face pale and drawn. He was wheezing, his breath coming in short gasps. Saliva dribbled from the corner of his mouth.

Alan sat on the chair next to his bed, and reaching across took his hand. Jim squeezed it. He reached across for a tissue and wiped his chin. He turned slightly to Grace and reading his face she went and sat in the chair on Jim's other side. She took his hand and he squeezed hers as well.

The three of them sat there in silence for a good half hour or more, until abruptly Jim seemed to relax, and he smiled and his breath became even. The nurse came over to check his pulse, and then said softly that maybe they should let him have his sleep. Rodney was perched on the end of the bed by then, Paddie still holding him by one hand even though he had nodded off again.

They trooped out and went inside the house. Ken stood as they came in through the door and as they sat at the big old dining table went across to the fridge for cold beer. He glanced back in askance, whether Grace or Rodney might want a soft drink, or cordial, or cold water. They both went for lemon cordial.

Alan sitting there reached across and picked up a spent rifle round, and while Ken was busy in the kitchen toyed with it; turning it around and about in his fingers.

When he came over with the tray of drinks and sat down, he looked up suddenly and asked him, "What I've been going to ask you, Uncle Ken, but keep forgetting, is what sort of round is that?"

The other took it and turned it around. He looked at the end, next to the primer, then leaned forward to show him.

"See there, son? That stamping on there? It's a .243 marksman round."

"Really? Do you mean, like sniper's use?"

"No, it's not a military calibre. I don't even know that roo shooters use them much; generally they'll use a .222 or .223. I know a couple of the fellas who use a .17, mostly foxes, eh?"

"Know anyone with a rifle like that, that fires them?"

"Yes, I do. Want me to show you sometime?"

81

"Ah, later. Not now. Wait until Christmas, alright. You can show me then. Will that be all right, show me then, Christmas I mean?"

"Sure. Take a few shots, if you like, see how good you are."

He glanced up at him.

"You're a good shot, eh? Uncle Ken. Andy reckons, anyway. He said you're a state champion, but maybe he was bullshitting to me."

"No, it's not bullshit. Show you my trophies too if you like."

"So you can shoot."

"Yes, sure. Why do you ask?"

"Because I want to know why you shot Barry."

The others sat still, watching him.

"Because it was a job that had to be done, Alan. Just a job."

"No, that's not right. It's not just a job, it can't be. It was Dad's funeral, and you ruined it."

Ken looked at him.

"We've had this conversation, Alan. I'm not going over it with you again."

"You're not going to tell me, you mean."

"No. Pointless. You already know, mate, and you need to drop it."

Rodney and Grace were both glaring intently at him by this time. The air was tense, and he thought for a moment he might black out. He hadn't touched the beer but his head swam. There was something else happening.

From some far distant corner of his mind, from over the horizon somewhere, out of the sky, there came a keening and a wailing.

The nurse came in through the door, but he only saw her through a dim haze at the edge of his vision; dimly aware that she was saying something to them, something about Poppy, and old Paddie.

All he could remember later was crying his heart out, sobbing his soul away, and Grace there cradling his head gently against her breast, rocking him back and forth, crooning to him, her own tears spilling and mixing with his down his cheeks and neck and chest, both of them.

Chapter Eighteen

Mum was there. She wasn't saying anything, busy and proficient as usual. On short notice she had simply closed the hotel declaring a death in the family, offering to refund all deposits and bus fares. It wasn't at all like Stan's funeral, and Bad Barry's, or the short service for Jack Hanley, within a local state of emergency almost, and police everywhere restricting through traffic.

Jim Forrestal as a gentleman and pioneer cattleman was legendary. Paddie Patjarrli Miller was for so long the most senior lawman, right across. The two of them were tribal brothers. They had lived and died together, for over three generations holding the entire southeast region in thrall to their wisdom and common sense. The whole region would be coming in, with more again from across the border and the desert proper to the northeast.

Nobody knew how old they were, either of them; most guessing between 87 and 100, though a lot of them saying an Aboriginal doesn't live anywhere near that long, the dates must be wrong, until somebody dug up an old title deed stating that Jim had taken out his first pastoral lease way back in 1930, at the start of the depression and he got it cheap, and he was of legal age to sign it. That meant he was born in 1909 or before, which made him at least 103. He and Patjarrli were about the same age then, give or take a few years; there was a grainy old black and white photo of them together, so old Paddie was closer to 100, late 90s anyway. That was sufficient to settle the matter.

Valerie was seriously pissed off. She had just arrived in Perth to have Sam pick her up at the railway station, not saying much to her, before arriving at their townhouse to find Danny and his mates had taken over. She saw straight away that he was now gay and during the daytime had the whole place to himself, the cheeky little prick, but didn't say anything even to Sam. She certainly wasn't going to tell Evie, or anybody else for that matter. Let him sort his own shit.

Then early afternoon, just after lunch, the phone rang to tell them that old Poppy Jim Forrestal had passed away finally, and Paddie Miller, and she sat down and cried all afternoon.

By 10:00 she was back on the train again, except with Eddie this time, and Sam and Danny in another seat. When Alan and Grace picked them up from Lake Marnma next morning, not waiting for Nanna and Pop and not telling them, Grace took her aside and told her brother in no uncertain terms just to bugger off for a couple of days.

He started to protest but Alan grabbed his arm and pulled him away, then with a quick glance at Sam climbed into the front of the car with him while the two girls sat way down the back by themselves.

The moment they pulled up in front of the Home Lake homestead, without a backward glance she disappeared inside with her, determined not to allow anyone near her, to chastise her or punish her, when the situation was already difficult enough. She made Eddie go and sleep in the men's quarters, in his old room that was his while he was jackerooing, except he could come up to the homestead for his meals.

Within the day people started arriving in long convoys, and buses, and light aircraft circling overhead before touching down on the airstrip. While expected, the deaths of the two most senior Law Men across both cultures throughout southwest-central Australia was a very big thing. Over the next few days there could be as many as 5-6,000 mouths there for them to feed and they'd better get themselves organised. While the bulk of them would disperse again once the funerals were over, within the week at the outside, the big tribal meetings would be going on for over a month or more.

The moment Bunna arrived with a truck load of stores from the hotel, towing the chiller van packed with meat carcases, he hunted Eddie out to help him and together with a few of the older more experienced hands they cleared out the big old station meat house and set up shop. Later in the day, a bit past mid-afternoon, an air freighter arrived loaded with groceries, vegetables and fresh fruit, followed by another that came in to land the moment the first plane took off again, carrying a full load of beer, wine, and single malt Scotch whisky.

By nightfall of the third day the campfires stretched out to the horizon, the smoke haze lit up and despite being a cloudless night the stars obscured by the soft afterglow.

They met the State Premier, and the Minister for Agriculture, and the Member for Kalgoorlie, the Member for Eyre, and a gaggle of MLCs for the Mining and Pastoral Region, the Chairman of the Pastoralists and Graziers Association, and the President of the Cattleman's Association, and the rest of them. Blah blah blah blah blah.

They went along serried ranks of painted and feathered desert elders and shook hands, and were smoked and rubbed with sweat, then in their turn taken aside and stripped and clad in loin cloths, and painted up to dance alongside their tribal brothers and sisters during the traditional ceremony, once the Christian whitefella bit was out of the way and the official party sat watching the spectacle.

Afterwards they all joined for drinks and refreshments, before the party climbed back into the government jet waiting for them on the airstrip and flew off, back to their official duties. It was an honour, Alan thought watching the plane climb straight up into the sky and disappear into the bright hot sun, but it's not something he wanted to be bothered too much about.

Around 11:00 that night Grace leaned in close to Alan, hand in his lap, and said quietly to him that she wanted to clear out back to Perth with Valerie; the sooner they could get away the better, otherwise there could be trouble. She didn't need it.

He agreed with her. Straight away he spoke to Eddie, and Rodney, letting them know to have their gear ready, then after a moment's thought went across and told Mum, then Sam. It was OK with them. Sam wanted to stay for the remainder of the week or so, to catch up with old friends, and help Bunna and the others get back down to Ballard and re-open the hotel. And see his wife, and have a long talk with her about the girls; not knowing at the time about Danny. He would take the train back.

Reuben wanted to return to Walilya once some of the meetings were out of the way; he might be here for a few weeks, with the old fellas.

At the first glimmer of dawn then, the moment they could more or less see their way, the five of them were at the fuel pump filling the tank.

Once away, off the gravel road across the station property itself and onto the sealed main road where they could hear themselves think above the teeth-chattering road noise, Valerie leaned forward and told them about Danny.

Nobody was surprised. He had always been too much of a giggler, especially in the shower; a bit too prone since he was 10 or 11 to playing with himself in front of the others, waggling his hips and jiggling his pee-pee about, joking and laughing about it.

Only Rodney said he didn't want him to come into the bathroom with him anymore; he didn't like Danny looking at him the way he did, and saying things, making jokes. Alan and Eddie didn't care either way, they already had him sorted. Right there and then they

87

were both thinking more about who his new boyfriend might be, and how they'd all manage to get along together.

Neither of them wanted him off the footie squad either. He was a very good player, very fast and agile; seriously able to handle the ball under pressure. Now that it was summer and they were spending more time at the swimming pool, he was taking his laps more seriously as well. Maybe they could recruit the new guy, whoever he was.

PART THREE

Chapter Nineteen

As luck would have it, the neighbouring townhouse appeared on the market. Suddenly there was a For Sale sign on the lawn out front. The owner had cash-flow problems with his business and needed to liquidate some of his assets. When Alan discovered he owned the third house on the block as well, he made him an offer for both of them but he only wanted to sell the one, except if he was happy to rent the third house on a long lease that would help a lot. Dodgy tenants had always been a major headache for him, and part of his financial difficulties.

They found themselves with far too much room now. Alan thought about it, and in the end declined the offer; taking only the one house that was for sale. In the end he agreed to manage the place; if they were to be looking after the two houses it might as well be three, and collect the rent and see to maintenance, while Sam was more than happy to tend the garden. Anyway he had a second garage now to park the car.

Immediately on settlement Sam had the boys help him demolish the dividing fence between the two back yards, and promptly began digging up the other yard to plant vegetables and fruit trees. Then he built a chook yard along the old boundary line with a duck pen on the side facing the other house, and as afterthought a pigeon loft at the end. Back in Seventh Heaven, he turned around and employed a registered doctor part-time to help run the clinic, and worked only every other day now instead of full time.

They had expected Danny's new boyfriend to be a spotty teenager still living at home with his parents, but he was twenty already. Valerie hadn't paid much attention to him, not thinking he was older than the others because he didn't look it. He was a qualified chef from Mauritius working in the city, with a French father and local mother like Monique, and a very good cook. He was very happy to pay rent for the room he now shared, it seemed, with Danny.

His name was Varun. Unlike Danny he wasn't queer about things, very steady and sensible, and Danny had settled down a lot with him. He just didn't play football, but worked night shift in the restaurant so nobody saw him much apart from Mondays and Tuesdays when he had his days off. Rodney didn't like him, and he didn't want to be bothered with Danny any more either, so after some discussion they both moved into the house next door with Eddie and Valerie.

With the extra space Sam kicked Rodney out of his room and he moved in with Reuben, who took over pretty much from Sam teaching him and supervising his homework.

Alan learned quite a lot about Sam during this time, no longer subject to his ministrations and able to stand back and observe. At his first opportunity, without making a fuss, the doctor called Danny into his room and give him a thorough medical examination, talking quietly to him all the while, asking him questions and noting his answers. He took blood tests, and examined his penis, then turned him around for an anal before standing him back up, indicating he could dress.

Danny came and told him about it later, him and Grace. Varun was still at work and wouldn't be home until the small hours, and he wanted to talk to somebody about it; reassure them. It was no problem; it was just nice. There was not much they could say, beyond thanking him for the confidence and trust. He was too shy to say anything to Varun; he didn't want him to think he didn't trust him or believe him, and asked Alan to let him know he should visit Dr Zhang and have a check-up too.

Better for them both. Better for everybody.

When he left Grace told Alan that her father had had a long talk with Valerie as well, not worrying so much about Eddie since he had already well educated him, and gave her some good contraceptive advice, and prolonged instruction on the rules of marriage, and on devotion and keeping the good name of the family. He needn't have worried, she was good; merely disoriented and lonely, caught up in the middle of all these arrangements without anyone ever asking her what she wanted or how she felt, and upset that she'd been given a hiding for her indiscretion when all she had wanted was to be with someone she loved.

He looked at Eddie with new eyes from then on too, and Grace, appreciating very much better what Reuben had said about two roads, except Chinese and Aboriginal; Asiatic, Oriental, with the whitefella way, its irregular, superficial Anglophone lingua franca aside, and without it being apparent, very much taking the back seat. He could see their mother Veronica's good reason for entrusting her husband so with her children when the whitefella had for generations simply failed them.

It gave him pause to think back to when he was just short of 12, and newly arrived Grace had taken his hand and swam uncovered and fun-filled and innocent with him out there in the desert waterhole there under the looming rock face of the breakaway, and her brother's and her mother's reactions once they were discovered, and Sam gently and patiently intervening the way he did.

He worried long and hard that without all the fuss they might have just been friends, that she tied herself to him to save face, but when she asked him what he was thinking about and he told her, she put her fingers to his lips and said softly, "No, I am in love with you the first time. I only ever thought, this is the boy for me. I only wanted to be with you. That was it. Don't think like that, Alan, it's not true. You are not fair to yourself, and you're not being fair to me. You don't see yourself the way I do, the way we do. Maybe it is true, you know, you are so like your father; you don't see yourself the way other people do. You look in the mirror and see different."

Under the shower after some good long laps at the swimming pool with Reuben and Danny, and Eddie, he mentioned what she'd said to him. They all nodded as one, grinning shyly at him, because they liked him, and said to him, "Yeah, that's right. Trouble with you whitefellas, eh?"

By the end of the next week Sam began to notice him. There was a new sadness about him.

"Alan," he said to him. "No ploblem. No worry so much."

"Sam," he turned and said to him, "if there's no problem, why is there a problem."

The old man stood up from his digging, and leaned on his shovel.

"Ah, now you are philosopher. OK. I can ask you, 'why is there life?' Why are you alive? Why you have all this 'stuff', you call it. What's going on?"

"What?"

Sam gazed across at him, then turned back to his digging.

"What, Sam? *Yuèmŭ*. What are you talking about?"

"Ha." Sam stood straight again, turning back to him. "How long I been teaching you, Alan?"

"Teaching me? Music? Um, six years."

"No. I never teaching you music. You alleady play music. What I teaching you?"

"Breathing. Alright, yes, breathing. You've been teaching me how to breathe properly."

"What happen you stop breathing?"

"Well, you'd be dead."

93

"What happen if not breathing properly?"

"You get sick."

"What happen when you sick?"

"Well, um, your life is pretty miserable, isn't it?"

"*Hou-ah*! You not so stupid. No Ploblem. Come, get some ekk. Chook laying ekk. Duck ekk, we make salt duck ekk. I teach you make salt duck ekk. So delicious."

Chapter Twenty

Most weekdays for the rest of summer the eight of them went swimming, and Mondays and Tuesdays Varun gave them all a break from cooking by preparing their meal himself. He didn't mind, he simply loved food and catering. He had worked in Paris, and proved to be something of an emerging authority on world cuisine, and full of jokes and stories. He and Alan got together and clearing an extended garden bed along the long wall that ran under both kitchen windows planted Mediterranean herbs that filled the houses with their pungent scent whenever the sun shone on them, with insects busily humming, and chickens clucking, and ducks quacking, and pigeons cooing endlessly.

They took eggs and fresh vegetables to their neighbours, in the other townhouse as well as the people next door, on the other side of the fence. It was nice. Looking after the small cluster of townhouses reawakened the yearning in him to be back helping to run a big hotel. He was grumpy with his mother over it, but maybe she was right and he wasn't old enough yet. Maybe he simply had to let go finally and concede that it was her job, her life, and he just happened to be born into it rather than work for it.

The old guys were a great bunch. He never saw Mr Carpenter again and nobody knew where he'd got to, and he didn't ask. The rest of them were all retired, in their third childhood and full of fun. They behaved a bit like an Old Farts bikie gang, but in vans instead of on motorbikes, with no plans and no schedule. Suddenly they would all just rock up, instruments and gear in a trailer behind the bus and the rest packed into the van, off somewhere without notice.

As often they would end up out in the bush somewhere, beside a river, and simply pile out and start playing jazz, and rhythm and blues, and bluegrass sometimes, and old 1920s jug band stuff with washboards and banjos if they were short on players that weekend.

When it was hot during the early afternoon they swam in the cool water. As it grew too dark to play they weren't allowed to light a fire because of the bushfire ban in place, so they gathered around the trailer and cooked steak and stew and served up great bowls of fresh garden salad, and drank beer, and before long just rolled out on their swags to sleep under the stars.

Having the boys with them, with their talent and youthfulness and pretty girlfriends, and the girls with their lovely singing voices and freshness and readiness to laugh; all of them respectful and well-mannered, for the old guys made that summer a truly great summer.

Rodney shifting back into the old boys' room with Reuben the moment he was back in from the desert marked another subtle shift in the household. Where he had bonded closely with Alan and to a lesser extent with Sam, now he was being more himself. Reuben wouldn't have put up with it anyway, but that was beside the point.

He was teaching him language.

Every day Rodney would take the crossword page out of the newspaper and sit there doing it, quietly leaving the unfinished words he found too hard there on the dining table for him, and in turn Alan who would complete the thing, then Rodney sat there thinking about his answers and the way the puzzle fit together; never saying anything about it.

As they found a spare moment they would walk together all the way down to the river, through the parks and into the bush proper, most of the time just sitting in the shade occasionally saying something to one another in their language, trying to get Alan to follow the conversation.

When Grace found out what they were doing she told her father she wanted to take a break from working at the clinic, and Valerie

96

came with her. With Valerie came Eddie, and with Eddie came Danny.

Eddie knew what the problem was with Alan. He'd crossed the Nullarbor and the southern edge of the desert on horseback with him, delivering him to the elders coming out of Walilya to meet them, back then, after his father died and brief flash of war hit Ballard; trying to get him to cry out his grief at his loss but only partly succeeding with him.

He'd been watching him closely for the whole of the five years since, not saying anything to anybody about it. His *tjamu* Frank Patjarrli didn't mention it because he didn't need to; Alan was *Katepa* as far as he was concerned who didn't know anything. He was that *pirranpa* boy at the hotel; that new one who could play trumpet but didn't have anyone to look after him properly. Only sometimes he and Andy Yatjimarra would sit and think it over, as Dan and Harry Forrestal would sit and mull over the likes of this unexpected Cameron nephew of theirs.

Tribally, even though there was less than a year in age between them, Reuben was his senior by a huge margin. It was not his place to speak. Reuben was a properly clever fella. He would become *wati*, and in time *tjilpi*. In time he would outrank that Yatjimarra, independent of their far greater age difference. Reuben was destined to be a teacher, and leader, and in such matters since that old *kunmangara* passed away had the respect and command of the most senior desert elders. Mr Baxter was personally overseeing his progress in whitefella business, as was the Home Lake station manager and now owner Harold Forrestal, and his own father properly Dr Sam Zhang Huá-wei.

He didn't have to ask, he knew.

Chapter Twenty One

There was a small sandy beach there in the inside bend of the broad flowing river quite a way upstream before it made its slow meandering way through the central city proper. Far across the shimmering water there appeared to be a golf course or something with trees scattered about, with a high chain-mail fence topped with razor wire around it. On that far side were small boat moorings by the look of it, with a narrow path or vehicle track between the fence and the river. It was too far across to see properly.

On this side there was a fair bit of trash lying about in the undergrowth, cold campfires and debris; old derelicts sleeping there sometimes, or kids over summer, or young lovers perhaps. It had that feel about it. The narrow path from the park down through the bush behind them was clear though overgrown in places. It didn't seem like a lot of people were using the place lately, and they had it to themselves.

They all took their bathers and changed into them for swimming just in case. Rodney like the older boys simply wore a baggy old pair of shorts while Danny didn't quite surprise everybody as he wished to by coming out in new purple hipster speedos that barely covered him, yet perfectly matched his dark velvet skin. While the impact on them wasn't what he wanted; they all knew him too well, they had to admit he had developed a nice body.

Grace asked him why he shouldn't think about becoming a model, but he grinned at that and said quietly that he had already enrolled ahead at the Performing Arts Academy, depending on his school results this coming year. That didn't surprise any of them either. A lot of their young people were now in film and media. Millennia of oral, performative culture had bred into them a natural talent with its own spontaneous expression.

Danny in particular was not only a fine athlete and a good competitive swimmer once he got used to there being so much water around, he was one of their best young dancers. Rodney liked to dance too, his body lithe and supple, except Reuben sitting there on the sand next to Alan chastised him for mucking around when he should be learning the proper dance steps, and the proper stories behind them. Disrespectful.

They were speaking in language and Alan had to ask what they were talking about.

As one they all turned to gaze at him, with the same startled frown. For over five years he had simply been one of them, speaking like them in rough pigeon much of the time, picking it up as kids do, and in more formal and polite English when they were at work or in school. While they knew it at one level, at another it hadn't properly occurred to any of them that he wasn't really one of them and had no real knowledge of their culture or language; their way of looking at the world, and of interacting with the world, except Eddie who had said nothing about it anyway.

Alan sat there on the sand oblivious, it only beginning to dawn on him that something else was happening. Grace glanced across at Reuben, who nodded in understanding, but then Eddie spoke in English; holding his hand up slightly to Reuben to let him speak.

He let him go. They all understood he knew Alan better than anybody, better than Grace in so many respects.

"Alan," he said softly, "up north, you know, that Wandjina there?"

"Wandjina? Yeah. What about it? Are they talking about Wandjina?"

"No. Listen. That Wandjina, that one, got no mouth. Big eyes, see everything, feel everything, not saying anything, just thinking.

Not that one, our mob; different culture, but like that. People like that. First, before language."

Alan was perceptive enough by now to realise he was having something explained to him.

After a long moment Reuben asked him, "Alan, what can you see, over there?"

He inclined his face slightly across the river, pointing with his lips.

Alan turned the top part of his body half about, gazing right across.

"Ah," he said, a short pause later, "that long fence. I don't know what; resort, golf course maybe. Track on this side, look, there's a car driving along. Those boats, um, I don't think they're fishing boats, maybe security, eh?"

He turned back to them. Valerie was looking intently at him.

"What you see there, Alan?" she cocked her head in the other direction.

He turned around to look. He scanned the understorey. Small birds flitted about, and more again in the treetops. As he flicked his eyes across the middle storey a small movement caught his eye. Something dashed behind one of the trunks, then reappeared slightly on the other side, head out peering at him.

He smiled and smiled, "Look. There. Goanna. What do you call that one?"

Without turning to look at it Reuben said, "Tinka. Not the same; tree goanna, this one. Sand goanna different one."

"*Kanyininpa*," Valerie said, almost inaudibly.

"What does that mean?"

"Ah, it means 'connectedness', Alan," Grace replied softly. "It means, 'holding responsibility'. We mean, looking after country, looking after one another. You can see like we do. But I thought that anyway. We were just checking. Old people want to know; other side mob."

"Yeah, OK. What does that mean? What are you saying?"

"It means, now you can learn language; you can understand what the words mean. You are not a little boy anymore. Now somebody will start properly teaching you language, if you want."

"My sister is trying to say, words aren't just words. They have a meaning," Eddie interrupted. "She is saying you can see our meaning so now you can learn the words. But your whitefella books are all just words. That's why we can't follow them, our people, not properly. We need you to help us with them."

He glanced back toward the trees. The goanna had made its way further up into the branches, forked tongue flicking in and out tasting the air for whatever there was to be had.

"So, really, I'm a sort of conduit for you?"

"Eh? What does that mean? That word."

"Pipeline. Gateway, you know, access."

The others glanced at one another, anxiously now. The idea was foreign to them, alien.

"They mean we need you to help us understand *Katepa*," Rodney spoke for the first time.

He turned to him. He liked him a lot, and he knew Rodney loved him a great deal, depended on him.

"What does that mean, *Katepa*?"

"It means, what I was saying before, opposite from Wandjina," Eddie broke in again. "Not the same, but like that. People can't see, can't feel, can't think, big mouth. Know nothing."

"But you've all been right through school with me. Your results are good, like mine, I know. Even you girls, home schooling, you still got good marks. How would I know *Katepa*? I am a whitefella, *pirranpa*; that's OK by me. But I'm not dumb, and I'm not ignorant. I have always been respectful and happy to learn. What's the matter?"

"Yeah, but it's all book learning, passing exams. We can remember it alright, but what does it mean? It's not connected with anything. It's schoolwork, eh?"

"Is that what this is all about? What are you going to do with it?"

"Yes."

"Why are you asking me? I don't know any of those people. I only know you fellas. How would I know? You say I don't properly understand blackfella way, maybe it's true, but you don't understand our way either. Don't worry so much. What Valerie said, *kanyini*. It's been good, we look after each other."

Reuben looked away across the river before glancing back at him.

"What are you going to do, you reckon?"

"Me? Well, I was thinking about doing Geology, Earth Sciences, maybe petrochemical, you know. Then I can go out bush again, and get paid for it, and help people. I was thinking about it, me and Uncle Ken, and your mother, eh? Except I don't want to be sitting on my arse, you know, between consulting jobs."

"Why don't you study music? Teach music?"

"Ah, too much fun, that's why. I don't know. Maybe we should open a jazz club or something, keep it for after work. I always wanted to run a nice hotel, but nobody will let me."

He glanced across at him, serious now. "Reuben, we are good mates, like brothers. I never had a brother, or a sister, only you mob, so I don't know, really. I can't say I know, like, if I had a brother and you are like him, if you know what I mean. Sometimes you say things that aren't fair, and I hear Eddie and Grace saying things to each other sometimes. I just think, that's the way brothers and sisters are to each other, so I don't worry about it much. But you say things about my houses and things that you shouldn't. I bought the next door townhouse to fit us all in, make room for everybody, without charging anyone anything. I'm not charging you rent, except Varun but he did anyway; it's all out of my pocket but you haven't thanked me for it, not any of you."

He paused for a moment before continuing. "You should, you know. Eddie's working now, and you have a scholarship, and Grace has a job. Sam helps me, but that's not the point. If we are going to be looking after each other you need to help me too. Not treat me all the time like I'm a lonely orphan or something, and you have to be looking after me. I'm somebody, I can stand on my own feet, but in our whitefella way."

"What I do have sorted out is we have to work hard all the time just like anybody, hunting, feeding your family, teaching your kids, looking after country, defending yourselves, everybody has to; it's all the same. I never saw any difference. You have your art and your culture to keep it all together, when you have enough time, and enough food, and everyone is happy. So have we, almost, except we have our business but our art has been stolen, appropriated by the wankers. It's all politics, not beauty or expression. I don't want to play that tune, that's all. Otherwise, it's just like everybody."

He looked at Rodney, then at Valerie and Eddie.

103

"Sam told me about a lot of things. I agree with him. And that *kunmangara*, that old one, your side, finish up now, he told me about *tjukurrpa*; my granny told me about *tjukurrpa*, so I know that much. But me, personally, I have only ever spent a few months at a time out there. All my life I've lived in the city, really; at the Federal Hotel, then at Bridgefield. Now we're all here."

"I understand Danny wanting to be a model and an actor. He's a good musician, and a good dancer. He's a good artist too, maybe he can design my supper club for me. I'm not sure about the rest of it; that's his business."

"All I am really, is a cornet player. I can play trumpet. It's silly when you think about it, just blowing into different bits of plumbing, eh? I have to work really hard at everything else."

"I don't want to talk about it anymore."

But then he turned and said something else, grumpy now, annoyed with them.

"Yes I will, sorry. You talk about two roads, but not properly. You checking me but I never worry about you. It's not all language and art and culture, it's everything. I'm really busy most of the time, not because I'm not looking. You don't think, I have all those houses now that I have to look after; all those people living in them that I don't even know, but I still have to look after them too. That's country. You should come with me and listen when I have a meeting with Uncle Greg. All that money that has to be managed, all those investments. It's all abstract, all of it, not connected. I have to stand back from it, be objective, and be fair. You mob can sit around and connect and talk about things, talk to one another, decide what to do; decide who is your mob and who isn't. I don't have that luxury. I have to do all my business myself. And I still have to sit my exams at school, and get into university."

"It doesn't matter, like Uncle Ken said to me; the map is not the territory. Sam says the same thing, sort of. Tell those old people that. Somebody else tell them."

Chapter Twenty Two

There were letters there for them on the dining table, he and Reuben. They knew what they were. He didn't open his straight away.

Varun was cooking dinner tonight. Danny felt terrible and wanted to make things up to him; persuaded Varun that he should help pay rent for the room too, though he'd said several times he wasn't that worried about it.

He was out in the back yard collecting squabs from the pigeon loft, a basket full of them; depleting their stock. They were all getting a bit big anyway, nearly a month old, and some of the breeders were ready to lay again. He'd tossed a coin with Rodney to see who got the job to chop their heads off and bleed them, and who had to pluck them, and he lost. He helped him anyway, it was just a bit of fun to ease a mucky job, and they soon had them all done.

They were large birds because Sam had selected French Red Carneaux crossed with American White Kings as breeding stock, so 15 were enough to feed the nine of them. Varun used a fairly simple recipe that brought out their full flavour, using shallots, thyme and lemon with salt and pepper in butter, smearing the paste up under the breast skin and around between the legs with his finger before browning them in a hot pan and placing them in a baking dish in the oven.

He served them up with potato wedges and fresh garden salad; always their favourite, with canned lychees and ice cream for their sweet. It made Alan think maybe they should make it their signature dish, once he opens his supper club, though as he thought about it suddenly he remembered his letter was there.

They were all looking at him as he read it, but without thinking he put it away again.

"What?" Grace wanted to know.

"Ah, yeah, science faculty; Earth Sciences."

Chapter Twenty Three

What changed Valerie's mind was Orientation Day. She thought university was going to be like school, all regimentation and homework, and standing around being bored despite her consistent grades, when her body ached to be a wife and a mother, and to look after children. The only reason she had enrolled at Forrest College with Grace and Danny was because otherwise she'd be home all day by herself. While her academic record was in the upper rank she didn't want to be stuck in school the rest of her life; the way she was thinking about it.

Eddie couldn't get away from work, but Grace and Danny were excused from class because it was University O-Day. Rodney decided to tag along regardless.

Getting off the bus together they joined the crowd. They happily toured the gymnasium and the music school, and the theatres and the Arts Building, and Law and Psychology, through the Guild Village, but when Alan headed across the broad expanse of lawn toward the Science Faculty Reuben demurred. He knew then it may be a parting of ways for them.

Reuben was being funded separately. Mum and Uncle Greg had stepped in when they realised there was a problem with his mother's trust fund, and the way her proceeds from the gold mining tenements were being managed. Cash had been leaking out everywhere with one thing or another and the principal slowly diminishing. It was OK, they understood the priorities, but the capital sum still had to be managed else they'd end up right back where they started.

Because of that, over the period they had transferred Danny especially back to the state grants system, keeping him on *Abstudy*, while he as well as Eddie happily agreed to pay rent at the house, and Mum and Sam chipped in for the rest. There was no hiding the steady profitability of the Ballard Hotel and the roadhouse, though it was not something they wanted to be doing. They wanted to show that good profit was being invested properly, and supporting the community.

Rodney was fascinated by the rocks in the Geology Museum, running his fingers along the glass naming them all as he went, reading the words on the labels and then speaking them in his own language, rolling them around on his tongue. In a world of his own almost.

Alan stood watching him, and he turned sensing him there, smiling shyly back up at him. That skinny little boy was a real treasure.

The Anthropology Museum was something of a challenge. The girls were upset at some of the things there, but the guy in charge was good, explaining the reason for the displays, the need to be educating people; asking them about their study plans. As he spoke something kept distracting him, making them all alert, slightly nervous. Rodney kept tugging at Alan's shirt sleeve, causing him to look down.

Finally the museum curator spoke to him, firstly in language, calling him *tjamu*, *tjitji*, then looking up suddenly said in English, "Rodney, isn't it? Rodney Cousens. Sorry, I didn't recognise him. He's a big boy now. I call this little boy grandson. That mother daughter belong me. What are you doing here?"

"How do you know Rodney?" Alan wanted to know.

"Ah, Dr Matheson. John Matheson. I work with the Pukuratju outstation mob. I wrote my doctoral thesis on them; on the cultural importance of the site and the need to recognise it, and resource the outstation. It was a few years ago now, how long? We were trying to get supplies delivered but when we got there all the kids were gone. All that kid mob. Nobody told us what happened to them."

His face reddened, profoundly angry of a sudden, jaw clenched, then looking into the distance cooled off again and taking a breath turned back to them, frowning quizzically.

"What name you mob? What place you from, eh?"

"I know you, Dr Matheson," Grace said softly. "I know who you are. Yes, I remember you, when I was little. My name is Grace Zhang, Ballard side. My father is Dr Zhang Huá-wei. This boy Alan, husband belong me . . . Alan Cameron. His mother Elsie Cameron, grandfather Jim Forrestal belong Lake Marnma. This one Valerie Scott. This boy Danny Scott. Another boy Reuben Scott, starting this year with Alan, but he looking at Arts Building, eh . . . Education Building. Teddy Scott mob, all this mob, belong Walilya . . . Yatjimarra cousin, right across. You been working with Aadhira Jayaraman, eh? Dr Jayaraman; Walilya clinic, is that right?"

But the curator had stopped hearing what she was saying to him. He was staring at Alan.

"Alan Cameron. You're the cornet player. Bridgefield Grammar. The pilot access program; Teddy Scott's early childhood program. And here you are, by God, you got in."

"How on earth did you find Rodney? How did he come to be with you?"

"I don't know, he just sort of, you know, found us. We've been looking after him. He'll be in Year 7 this year, but he's still doing home schooling, more or less. Sam is teaching him; Grace's father, Sam Zhang. Grace won't be here until next year . . . Medicine . . . she has to finish Year 12 first . . . her and Valerie. Danny wants to get into the Performing Arts Academy."

"So, what are you enrolled in, Music?"

"No. I'm not studying music. Earth Sciences . . . Geology."

"And Eddie, Eddie Cheong, what's he doing?"

"Ah, got a job, eh? He's working out at Midland, stock and station agent . . . cattle buyer. He's Valerie's bloke, you know. Promise. Husband."

"Bless my soul. Well, bless my soul. Come with me, will you?"

He turned on his heel and called an assistant over to show people through the museum, then led the way through a back door into the huge building above.

The new program was much better. Nobody had told them anything; said anything until now, let them know what options were available. Valerie really should have been in with them from the beginning, and Evie and Frances for that matter. All that worry about her and Eddie was a load of bullshit. Nobody had made such a fuss about Alan and Grace, though they may have but couldn't do much about it because of all those responsible for them only Veronica was properly a senior tribal woman, and Sam and Elsie were powerful figures in the surrounding cosmos.

It wasn't that the promise was wrong-way, only that they were too young; except the big wide world had intervened and buggered everything up. He smiled ruefully, realising he hadn't been the conduit but the bait, and it was all his own doing when he lost his temper and throttled that little shit, the politician's brat, and cleared out from Bridgefield that first week he was there by himself.

It was all right for him. For their part, while he had been drawn into their kinship system, as does everybody coming close, it was to avoid confusion when addressing him, and speaking of him, rather than his actually being adopted as family in the proper sense. He thought about that quite a lot. He enjoyed freedoms not allowed the others, which they yearned for without quite realising yet the other restraints upon him. No free lunch either way.

What they decided to do, even though she was not yet 20 to qualify for mature-age entry, was enrol Valerie in the university's remote outreach program, and their mid-semester and mid-year orientation camps that she could go on separate from the others, to wean her off Grace to some degree and have her on her own feet as a student in her own right. For the remainder she would complete Year 12 at Forrest College with Grace and Danny.

If they wanted to, the two girls could attend the holiday revision programs and prepare their tertiary entry exams, mainly because they had been home schooled all the way through, or small bush schools lacking the rigour and discipline of the big city schools.

It was Rodney who was the real winner. They enrolled him straight away in a special primary school just off-campus where he could access enrichment and extension programs, then proceed to Year 8 directly next year under the university's Aim High program.

Sam provided his entire medical history referred to him by Aadhira Jayaraman, and once the school had examined him on his progress they realised he was a very clever boy who would attach to the school and enjoy the special attention, and gain benefit from it. Alan changed his schedule so they went off together every morning, then if he had a late lecture Rodney came across and sat in with him. If he wasn't there to escort him across the road when school finished, one of the teachers would bring him over.

Chapter Twenty Four

"Hey, Alan! Alan! Alan Cameron, isn't it?"

He turned to see who it was. Some guy running after him.

"Yeah, um, Guy, like Guy Prentice, Uni Jazz Club," he gasped once he caught up. "Alan, I'm told you play hell cornet. You know, any time you're in for a gig, eh?"

"Sure, yeah, OK." He looked him up and down.

"What are you studying?"

"Oh, what? Yeah, Engineering. Over there."

"Geology, Earth Sciences."

"Ah, right! Like, mining. I know your Uncle Ken Forrestal. Adjunct Lecturer. Smart guy!"

Alan glanced away, shaking his head. Bastard, eh? Dark horse that Ken, seriously. But Guy was still talking to him, bringing him back to the present.

"Les tells me you play Kaempfert, Alpert."

"Yes, I do. I like any swing sound, any of those shuffled eighth note pieces. And syncopating, you know, off beat, odd stresses, intuiting, connecting. What I mean is, remapping. Big Band is OK, or a quintet, but with orchestral backing, there's a subtlety to it, a nuance. Grace sings jazz really well, and blues; great range. Room for vocals?"

"Right! Friday then. Not the Tav, eh? Music School, over that way."

Guy kept looking at him, still breathless. "Like, Les tells me you have a Bach Stradivarius."

"Yes, I do. They gave me a *Wild Thing* short cornet too. I haven't played it much yet."

"A *Wild Thing*? Like, Flip Oakes? Wide mouth? Fuck. Creaming my pants already."

"What? No, don't do that."

"No! Yeah, you're right! Swing, eh? Soloist freedom. Bring the orchestra. Man, it's done."

Guy turned on his heel and rushed off. Alan gazed after him, then turned himself to cross the wide expanse of lawn toward the bus stop. Rodney would be waiting for him. He worried when he was late.

Crossing the lawn he thought about Ken. He couldn't get that spent .243 cartridge case out of his mind. He had dreamed about it so often now. Ken was lecturing here, in mining engineering, and he hadn't said the least word to him about it. That long shot he took, back then, popping Barry's eye out, from behind at 850 metres, and he was the only one who knew because he was the only one facing that direction, playing cornet, and without thinking worked it out, and was told to shut up about it. Not good enough.

He knew then that this business was never going to leave him alone. What was Sam saying to him all the time? The breathing. The meta-message. We've had this conversation before.

Rodney was there at the bus stop, gazing intently at him as he approached.

He was still thinking about that one shot. Exquisite, when you thought about it. Perfection, once you stood back away from the event, and saw it for what it was. A job needing to be done. Left eye or right eye. Neither would have been the ultimate, but what the heck.

Around 11:30 there was a scratching at the door and he murmured to it. It opened slightly and almost straight away he felt a weight on the edge of the bed. Grace turned over and spoke softly, and the weight shifted. After a moment Rodney's warm little body slid under the sheet between them.

"Roddie," he muttered eventually, restlessly. "It's too hot, mate. Go back to your own bed."

When no answer came he repeated himself.

Finally Grace said to him, "Turn the fan on, Alan, if you're hot."

"Alright, but no more after this."

He got up and turned the ceiling fan on, adjusting it to low.

Clambering sleepily back into the bed he said, "You're a big boy now, Roddie, properly; Year 7 boy. You can sleep in your own bed. Deal with it."

"Yes, alright," Grace replied patiently. "Tell him when he wakes up. I'll talk to him."

"He can hear me."

Chapter Twenty Five

When they got home on Friday the Internet man was there. Grace had let him in. He was an old telephone guy who used to lay long copper cabling, and electronics back in those days before everything became microchips. The girls didn't have a clue what he was talking about. Danny was off somewhere with his friends, and Reuben wasn't home yet.

What he was saying was that he was surprised the house had been wired up already, from new it looked like. The three townhouses were not that old, only four or five years, with wall plates in every room supplying both Ethernet and television sockets. The man had brought a ladder in and climbed up into the ceiling through the manhole, and he was trying to explain to them there was an old five-port switch up there plugged into a power point, still turned on.

Alan was curious. He went in next door and noticed that house had wall sockets as well, so he came back suggesting they look up in the ceiling of that house too. Same thing.

The man said he had a separate order for a modem in that house, until Alan told him they were both his houses, and they all lived there, sharing. He wanted to know, if the two houses were already wired up why did he need two modems?

"Well, you don't. If you want, I can run a patch cable through the brick wall up there and just connect the two networks. Save you a lot of money, paying for two separate accounts when you can do with the one."

"Is that right? Why do we need cables? I thought it was WiFi or something. I thought the signal wouldn't reach that far, if we only had one modem."

"Ah, cable is much faster. You can take your laptops into the garden if you like, pick up WiFi from there, it'll be strong enough. But if you're inside browsing the Net, cabling is 20,000 times faster."

"Really? Well, do that then. What about those switches up there, is that what you call them?"

"Yes, just network switches; that's all they do, route signals. They're a bit old, you might want to replace them, upgrade."

He turned to look at him, wanting to explain it.

"I can take those five-ports out and replace them with the one 24-port switch. Same quality as the Internet cafes use, if you have that many people to connect. There is plenty of slack cable up there, enough to reach. The new modem I brought with me is good for the job."

"OK, good, do it that way. Ah, and change it to a business account then."

He stopped and thought for a moment, then called out to Grace. She was outside with Rodney feeding the chooks and collecting eggs.

"Honey, we've been going to get you a laptop, eh? I need a new one. We'll go and get them. Rodney can have my old one."

"Isn't it a bit late? The shops will be closed."

"No, Friday, they'll be open until 7:00, or something. We can go now."

"Alright. Get one for Valerie too. She'll pay for it when her scholarship comes through. Is that OK? She needs one. She knows how to use them, from school, better than me."

The phone was ringing and Danny rose from the table to answer it.

"Ah, Alan, some guy says they've got a jam session going; said he told you about it. Wants to know if you forgot, eh?"

"Oh, yeah, shit, tell him sorry, we've been mucking around with computers. That's Guy, his name's Guy. I'll be there."

He looked around the table. "You guys in for a jam tonight?"

"That's not an Oakes wide mouth."

"No, it's my Salvation Army Bandmaster; played it since I was five. It'll do, just jamming, eh? Sounds real sweet. Ah, this is Danny, guitar, and Eddie over there, drums. Grace and Valerie do vocals. Reuben couldn't get here."

"Ah, yes, well, some people here heard you were coming tonight; want to hear you play."

"Sure, whatever. You told them, eh? So, let's play."

Danny nearly spoiled things by giggling, listening to him. He really was gay and couldn't contain himself. He knew what was coming. Some of the old Bridgefield boys were there, enrolled to study music. Alan had seen them from the car so instead of bringing the Oakes in with him picked up the old Bandmaster.

"Ah, need a trumpet," Alan was saying, "and a piano."

A couple of hands went up, and he pointed to them both before turning to wait until Eddie was set up. Finally Eddie gave him the nod, and turning to the others he said, "Right, Whipped Cream, eh?"

They hit it. Foot still tapping as they finished Alan said straight away, "OK, do it, Lollipops and Roses."

Nobody else knew what to expect, except Eddie on drums and Danny on guitar, so it took a moment for the others to catch on. They had enough leeway before the trumpet came in, then the trombones. Les was onto it.

Before they finished playing some of the students were already packing their instruments to leave, so he stopped there; raising an eyebrow in their direction.

"Fucking show-off, Cameron!" one of them was yelling. "Our parents pay a lot of money for us to come here and study music. You ruined our music program at Bridgefield with your smart-arse bullshit, now you're here!"

As they left Alan bent down and said to Rodney that he could go out to the car and bring his instruments in now. People were watching them. When Rodney returned with the two cases two of the others came up to them; two older, distinguished looking fellows.

"Alan," one of them said, "I am Professor Kovid. This is my colleague, Professor Edwards. Thank you for that."

"No worries. Just sorting those dickheads out. Hope you don't mind."

"Well, no, of course not. We are not having this conversation, of course, but you have saved us some embarrassment later. Good riddance. What we'd like to do is offer you a post with us as tutor. We are very interested in your technique."

"Me? Nah, I'm doing Geology. You should talk to Dr Zhang, he's the man."

"We have already spoken to him. He insists that it be you."

"Sam? Did he do that? Alright, let me think about it. I have to find my feet yet, you know; on campus, I mean."

"Sure, no problem. We'll talk again later."

"Alright, sometime, eh? Can we play some music now? What would you like?"

"Let's run through your repertoire, if you're agreeable. Let's just get an idea of what we have here."

Chapter Twenty Six

He should have known better than to argue with Sam, but he did anyway.

"Ha! Alan! Nobody can teach you music. Now you teach music, can learn music. Better."

"It's not that. Nothing to do with it. I just don't have time, that's all. I'm tired when I come in."

"Oh, that's it! So tired. Go straight to sleeping, can't make love with wife, can't get up in the morning! I give you some tonic."

"What? Of course I can. It's not that bad."

"So! Nothing more you can say."

Sam turned to face him. "Alan, you are not average player, you are great player, great human being, I keep telling you, evlybody telling you; getting better."

He didn't say anything much for a while, just stood there looking at the chooks pecking around in the yard, and through the wire to the ducks splashing about in their little pond that he and Rodney had made for them, from old bricks and left-over cement. It needed cleaning.

"Alright," he said finally. "Tell Mum I want them to form a trust or something to look after all the other stuff. You, and Mum and Greg, and somebody independent, not Ken. Also, ask Harold, he'll do it for me. He's smarter than any of them now. He's so much more like Poppy Jim than any of them still alive. Just because he's a big ugly lump of a stockman who no woman wants to marry they think he's stupid, but I want him as chairman. That's five, with my great uncle Harold the decider."

"If you do that for me, I'll teach music."

But Sam was down the other end of the garden by then, watering the long fragrant herb bed there under the kitchen window, chuckling to himself.

THE END

ABOUT THE AUTHOR

As an anthropologist, novelist and writer Gil Hardwick is a gifted and imaginative author. Over many years working as a field ethnographer in the vast Australian inland he has met real characters and had real-life adventures, bringing his personalities and his plots to vibrant life. Writing from life, he neither shies away from real social issues and at times confronting dilemmas.

Well worth reading.